MY BROTHER'S ENVY

The Reconciliation

J.L. Rose

GOOD2GO PUBLISHING

My Brother's Envy 3

Written by J.L. Rose
Cover Design: Davida Baldwin
Typesetter: Mychea
ISBN: 9781947340152
Copyright ©2017 Good2Go Publishing
Published 2017 by Good2Go Publishing
7311 W. Glass Lane • Laveen, AZ 85339
www.good2gopublishing.com
https://twitter.com/good2gobooks
G2G@good2gopublishing.com
www.facebook.com/good2gopublishing
www.instagram.com/good2gopublishing

DEDICATIONS

This book is dedicated to each and every one of my fans! I love you all!

~ J.L. Rose

Acknowledgements

Yo, we back at it, y'all! I first wanna say thank you to God, the Creator of everything and the one I know will never leave me or stop loving me. Also to my mom, Ludie Rose. You are my heart, and I love you above all women no matter who they may be. And to my pops, John L. Rose Sr. Dad, you're gonna be my best friend and hero forever. I love you, old man!

~ J.L. Rose

Prologue

Stephen King exited Supremely Divine with his wife, followed by their bodyguards. He escorted her over to their diamond-black Rolls-Royce Ghost. Once they got inside, he allowed her to lean in and lie against his chest. He then wrapped his arm around her and even kissed her forehead as their driver pulled away.

"Honey, I was thinking!" Stephen heard his wife say, looking down at her as she lifted her head from his chest.

He sat listening to her talk about them taking a trip somewhere away from Chicago just to relax and spend some time together.

"I tell you!"

Brrrr! Brrrr!

"Oh my God!" Melody King screamed as both she and Stephen heard the semi-automatic machine guns go off.

Stephen instinctively pushed his wife low as he pulled out his .38 from his side holster. He looked out the back window and saw the craziness as his driver was doing one hell of a job getting him and his wife away from the scene unharmed.

Once the driver slowed the car but was still driving at a good speed, Stephen helped his wife up and then put away his gun.

"Sweetheart, you all right?"

"Stephen, where are we?" Melody looked over and asked while nodding her head.

Stephen also looked around but didn't recognize the area. He was just about to call up to the driver, when the car suddenly stopped in the middle of a dark road.

"What the hell!" Stephen called out when the car locks activated.

~ ~ ~

Boss watched from the back seat of his Bentley with Rachell seated next to him as Joker climbed out and walked away from the Rolls-Royce Ghost. Boss then saw Black Widow and Savage appear out of the darkness.

"You may want to watch this!" Boss said to Rachell, pointing over in the direction of the Rolls.

Rachell followed Boss's instructions and began to smile once the woman and muscular man began filling the Rolls-Royce with bullets from their MAC-11 and AK-47.

Boss looked over at Rachell and saw the smile on her face. He called up front to Trigger and motioned for him to drive as he focused back to Rachell.

"So now that that's over, are you still questioning my father and my ability to build this business, or are you with us fully?"

"Lead the way, Boss!" Rachell told him, realizing that Chicago really had problems on its hands with ReSean Holmes, a.k.a. Boss.

MY BROTHER'S ENVY

The Reconciliation

1

Two hours later . . .

Boss stood out on the terrace overlooking the city and water when he heard the commotion from inside the penthouse. He didn't bother looking back since he was pretty certain who it was that was causing the turmoil. He heard the sliding glass door open behind him.

"You just had to do it, didn't you?" Malcolm Sr. asked with a tone that was laced with anger.

Upon hearing the sliding door shut, Boss remained staring out over the view until his father stepped up to the rail beside him.

"You plan on answering my question?" Malcolm asked his son while staring hard at him.

"You asked me to come up here for a reason!" Boss finally spoke up, looking over toward his father. "You know what I'm capable of and what I would do when I got here. Stephen King was a problem that interfered with our business plans. And now that problem is no longer a problem."

Malcolm shook his head as he now stared out at the view, and then sighed loudly.

"You do know there is likely to be a war because of this, right?"

"Between whom?"

Looking back to his son after the question was asked, Malcolm asked, "Boy! What the hell you mean between--?"

"Remember what you told me?" Boss interrupted his father as he looked over to meet his eyes. "Stephen King was a major player in things up here, which obviously meant he had enemies. Some he knew of, and some, I'm sure, he was not aware of but suspected. I'm sure everyone is going to have their own thoughts and feelings about who's responsible for his death. But I'm willing to bet that the person closest to him will be the main suspect, and why is that, Pops?"

"Power!" Malcolm answered, now understanding his son's madness.

"Exactly!" Boss stated with a small smile on his lips.

"Everyone knows Stephen King was backing Austin Jones; but as long as Stephen was alive and breathing, he remained the power in the city, which left Austin Jones just a student."

"So basically what you're saying is that because King is dead, everybody's attention will be focused on Austin Jones?" Malcolm asked with a knowing smile.

"Well, that, and it also leaves room for the smarter and stronger house to step into a position of power," Boss explained to his father with a smile.

Malcolm shook his head as he stared at his son.

"Boy, how old are you again?"

Boss heard a light knock and looked back at the sliding glass door to see Black Widow standing on the other side holding up his phone. Boss motioned for her to step outside onto the terrace.

"It's April calling," Black Widow informed Boss as he took the phone.

Boss conversed with April about his roxies connect and a few other things for a few minutes before he hung up. He then made another call to his boy Murder in Atlanta about his new shipment order. They spoke in code the entire conversation. He then hung up the phone and handed it back to Black Widow.

"Pops! I need to use the jet!" Boss informed his father before he turned around to face him directly.

"Not a problem!" Malcolm replied with a nod of the head. "I'll have Ike assign a driver to take you, and, I'm sure, Trigger, out to the airstrip."

~ ~ ~

Malcolm heard his cell phone ring just as Ike was driving him away from his son's penthouse. He dug out his phone and saw that Rachell Harris was calling.

"Hello!"

"Malcolm, you are not going to believe who just called me!" Rachell told him. But before she had even given him time to reply, she continued. "Austin Jones! He's called a meeting and wants me to come out to his building, so I'm guessing he's calling everyone."

"He hasn't called me!" Malcolm stated with a small smile on his face as thoughts of what Boss had told him only a few minutes ago crossed his mind again. "I'm pretty sure I won't be receiving that phone call though, since it's well known that Austin Jones and I are not fans of one another."

"Well, I'm not going if you're not going!"

"No! Go to the invitation!" Malcolm told her. "Just let me know what's going on and what Austin Jones has planned, because it's clear he's got something he's planning."

Malcolm hung up after speaking with Rachell for a few more minutes. He sat thinking for a brief moment, when his phone began to ring again. He looked down at the caller ID and saw Boss was now calling him.

"Yeah, son!"

"Pops! I was doing some thinking about what we discussed."

"Rachell just called about Jones just now," Malcolm cut his son off. "From what she just explained to me, Austin is calling a meeting and wants to discuss something."

"Has he called you yet?"

"That's not happening."

Boss remained quiet a few seconds and then asked, "Pops, where you going now?"

"Home. Why?"

"There's been a change of plans, Pops!" Boss said. "We're going to make a surprise visit at this meeting."

~ ~ ~

Rachell arrived at the meeting with her personal bodyguard and a team of fifteen security escorts, along with a backup team of twenty who waited outside of the building that was owned by Austin Jones. She allowed her bodyguard, Bruce, to lead the way.

They took the elevator up to the fourth floor, and then Rachell followed Bruce off of it along with four of her men, just as the others were stepping off two other elevators. She continued following her bodyguard up the long hallway to a double wooden door that was opened by two of Austin's men.

"Rachell Harris!" Austin announced from the front of the room as he stood at the head of the glass table that sat fourteen people.

He spotted her as soon as she and her bodyguard entered the room.

"We were waiting on you, Rachell. Have a seat and we will continue!"

Doing as she was told, Rachell took a seat at the far end of the table, with Bruce a few feet behind her against the wall. She then focused her attention on Austin.

"Now as I was just saying," Austin continued as he looked at the eight faces that sat around the table watching and waiting on him, "I'm sure you've all heard about Stephen King. He was suddenly murdered, which is unexplainable since each of us know how extremely difficult it was to get to him."

"Doesn't seem like it was all that difficult to me!" Tony Roosevelt spoke up, drawing attention from the other bosses.

"That may seem true, Tony!" Austin said, showing a small smile. "Whoever was lucky enough to get to him was just that—lucky! But as I said before, we have to continue with business. I think it's about time that we made a few changes as well."

Austin heard the commotion just before the office doors flew open and both of his security men he had positioned at the door came flying into the room. Austin and every other boss inside the room watched as a massively muscular man walked inside moments behind the two now unconscious security guards tossed to the floor. They were then followed inside first by a young man and then Malcolm, who stepped inside with a big smirk on his face.

"Gentlemen!" Malcolm stated before he nodded to Rachell, who returned a small smirk to him. "Ms. Harris."

After receiving a nod in return from Rachell, Malcolm continued with what he was saying.

"It seems like I wasn't invited to the meeting, and considering every family's head is present, I figure I should have been notified."

"You were phoned, and no answer was ever received," Austin explained. "Your men can wait out in the hall so we can continue with our discussion."

"Not happening!"

Austin shifted his gaze from Malcolm Sr. over to the

young man who stood alongside but slightly behind him.

"Who the hell are you?" Austin asked, with a balled-up face.

"Austin Perry Jones!" Boss began, pronouncing his full name as he stepped forward and slowly began strolling around the table. "It's amazing you don't know who I am, but I know exactly who you are. Father is Austin Perry Jones Sr., and your mother is Rebeka Scott, who isn't the woman your father is married to."

Malcolm Sr. was surprised as he stood staring at his son. He listened as his son began telling Austin's life history to everyone in the room, from where he went to school even to what STDs he had contracted. Malcolm smiled since he was very impressed with his son's approach and knowledge of Austin Jones.

"Enough!" Austin yelled, cutting off Boss as the boy continued walking toward him. "Who the hell are you, boy?"

Boss stopped directly in front of Austin.

"Can't you tell, Austin? Don't I look familiar to you, since you don't really care too much for my father, Malcolm

Warren Sr.!"

Gasps could be heard throughout the room, and Boss enjoyed the look that passed across Austin's face.

"Sit the fuck down!" Boss calmly said in a voice just loud enough only for Austin and him to hear.

"Who the fuck?"

"Now!" Boss barked, which caused Austin to jump in both shock and slight fear that showed on his face.

Austin held the green eyes of the young man who had an expression on his face that actually worried him a little. He then stepped back and slowly sat down in his seat at the head of the table.

"Now!" Boss began, once Austin was seated yet staring hatefully back at him.

Boss ignored the look as he then introduced himself and moved directly into the subject of business. He then offered everyone the choice of continuing business with the Warrens and Harrises, or taking their chances on going into business for themselves.

"What if two or three of us decide that we'd rather join

together than join this Warren and Harris collaboration?"

Boss looked up at the light-skinned, middle-aged drug boss.

"What's your name, sir?"

"Isaac Edwins!" he proudly responded as he began to continue, only for Boss to beat him to it.

"Well, Mr. Edwins, as I've said before, you as well as the rest of the men inside the room have the choice to either work with the Warrens and Harrises or for yourselves. But to speak truthfully, I cannot see any other organization succeeding once the Warren and Harris collaboration begins business. So this is the offer now to join us, because we're seeking to have greater business, make more money, and have a wider reach of buyers. In fact, Miami and Atlanta have already agreed to deal with us—and only us!"

Malcolm smiled proudly while watching his son conduct business and work the men in the room. They were locked on to every word that left Boss's mouth. Malcolm looked around at each of the men's faces and watched a few of them offer up nods of agreement and even some approving smiles.

"Malcolm, he is amazing!" Malcolm heard one of the drug bosses call out as he looked over at Rachell, who was leaning over toward him.

"He reminds me a little of you, Malcolm!" Rachell whispered in his ear. "He just has this energy and pull about him that makes you want to follow him, Malcolm. You've really taught him well!"

~ ~ ~

Malcolm sat through the entire meeting that Boss had completely taken over. He noticed how the other men began to get invested in the meeting and ask interesting questions, to which Boss answered and met their approval by the looks on their faces. Malcolm and Rachell then answered a few questions once the meeting was over.

Malcolm returned to Boss's Bentley, and then he, Rachell, and Boss stood outside the car and spoke with their team. Malcolm and Rachell's security guards surrounded them.

"What's up, Pops?" Boss asked when he noticed the way his father was looking over at him.

"I'm just proud of you, Son!" Malcolm told him. "You did good, Boss!"

"Malcolm, he did better than good!" Rachell spoke up with a smile. "You were amazing in there, Boss! Do you know how many of them approached me and asked if you were really a part of this collaboration that you had come up with?"

Boss allowed a small smile to appear on his face as the three of them stood and continued their talk.

"Can either of you tell me how many wars Austin has been a part of?" Boss changed up the conversation.

"A few!" Malcolm answered, staring back at Boss with a questioning look on his face.

"Just thinking about something," Boss replied as he noticed the looks on both his father's and Rachell's faces. "Do either of you have a contact in law enforcement?"

"I know a captain that used to deal with my husband, but now he deals with me!" Rachell informed Boss.

"Who's the tail for? Austin?" Malcolm asked, lowering his voice.

"And Isaac Edwins!" Boss added. "Inside the meeting, did either of you notice that other than Austin, Edwins continued speaking about building their own organization. And I caught their eyes and nods cutting back and forth at each other."

"I did notice it!" Rachell agreed.

"Yeah! I noticed it as well."

"They're plotting something!" Boss said with a certain tone.

"I'll get with my connect!" Rachell eagerly stated, digging out her cell phone.

~ ~ ~

Boss and Malcolm finally left the parking lot of Austin's building after talking out front for about forty-five minutes. They discussed a variety of topics before sitting in the back seat of the Bentley where both of them sat in deep thought until Boss broke the silence.

"Pops, what's up with you and my mom?"

Malcolm looked over at his son, who was staring directly at him.

Malcolm sighed loudly as he ran his hand over his short hair.

"I figured this conversation was coming sooner than later!"

"So, let's handle it then!" Boss told his father before he called up to Trigger, who was driving. "Bruh, roll up!"

Boss then turned his attention back to his father and listened as he began explaining first how he and Boss's mother had met and how they then decided to separate because of Malcolm Jr.'s mother becoming pregnant.

"Pops, look! Let's just get to the point! Are you and my mom getting back together or not?" Boss interrupted.

"Yeah, we is!"

"So what about Patricia?"

Malcolm sighed once more and then admitted, "I'll be truthful with you, son. I love Patricia, but I'm still in love with your mother; and we've discussed this already and both agreed that we would try doing us again."

Boss nodded his head at his father's words before he turned away and looked back out the window.

"How exactly do you know Patricia's name? Did you have me looked up?" Malcolm asked his son.

"Actually, I had Malcolm Jr. looked up!" Boss admitted. "You, Patricia, and Destiny were just extras."

Once he returned to his penthouse, and Malcolm and his security team had gone home, Boss got ready for his flight back to Miami. He then attempted to call Vanity to let her know that he was returning, only to receive her voice mail since he had forgotten about the time change difference.

2

Vanity heard her cell phone ring but ignored it since she had only gotten home a few hours earlier and was finally getting some rest. She rolled over onto her left side and was determined to get back to sleep, when, first, she felt arms wrap around her from the back and then she heard a voice.

"Ma! You not gonna answer that?"

Vanity completely woke up, and within moments she was screaming. She leapt out of the bed and was reaching for the burner that Boss made sure she kept close at hand.

"Vanity, what the hell is wrong with you?" Boss yelled over her screaming while ignoring the banger she was now pointing at him.

"What? What are you doing here?" Vanity blurted out, staring at Boss in both shock and disbelief.

"Last time I checked, I live here too!" Boss replied as he sat up in the bed and stared at her. "And how about aiming that gun someplace else, ma!"

Vanity lowered the gun but still stared at her man. She

finally got control of herself and set the gun down, only to look at the door.

"Boss!" Lloyd yelled as he and Tina stood at the bedroom door. "When'd you get back here?"

"A lil' while ago," Boss answered as he and Lloyd embraced each other.

He then looked over at Tina, who remained standing at the bedroom door simply staring at him.

"What up, lil' sis?"

Tina broke out in a smile after Boss spoke to her and called her his sister. She rushed over to the bed and hugged her big brother, whom she just recently found out was related to her.

"Boss, why didn't you tell me you was coming home?" Vanity asked as she climbed back into the bed beside her man.

"I tried to call before I left Chicago and again when I landed in Miami," he explained. "You never answered."

"I probably had my phone off," Vanity responded. "Me and Gigi had to drive out to the other club yesterday. There was a little problem, and then we had a meeting."

"Where was Princess?" Boss asked, losing all playfulness and becoming dead-ass serious as he stared at Vanity.

"Relax, Boss!" Vanity told him with a smile. "Both Princess and Butter drove with us, along with the security you assigned."

Boss relaxed after hearing what Vanity had just told him about Princess and Butter, before changing the subject.

"Lil' Man, you ready for your birthday?"

"I got a lil' something for both you and Tina!" Boss told him while smiling over at Tina. "Y'all go put something on, and we'll go check it out!"

Boss smiled as he watched both his sister and Lil' man rush from the bedroom. He then looked back over at Vanity to find her smiling and watching him. He leaned over and kissed her lips.

"I've got a few hours before I leave. How about getting some breakfast together?"

"We can do that now!" Vanity told Boss.

A mischievous smile soon began to appear on her face as she reached over between Boss's legs, gripped his manhood, and began stroking him through his silk boxers.

"You do know what we will be doing before you leave, right?"

"Yeah, I pretty much fully agree," Boss said as he slowly smiled back at Vanity.

~ ~ ~

After showering together and then getting dressed, Vanity and Boss met up with Lloyd and Tina, who were waiting and talking inside the den. Boss led his family from the penthouse to the elevator as the four of them rode down to the lobby.

"Lil' Man!" Boss called out as he and Vanity walked out of the front doors of the building behind Lloyd and Tina.

"Yeah!" Lloyd answered as he stopped and looked back at Boss, only to catch the keys that Boss had tossed to him. "What are these for?"

"Those!" Boss answered, nodding his head.

Lloyd looked in the direction that Boss nodded, only to

lock in on the gray metallic and black 2017 Porsche 911 Carrera and the crystal-white, pearl-metallic, drop-top Porsche 911 Carrera S Unveiled.

"Boss, you serious, man?" Lloyd said to Boss with a huge smile on his lips.

Boss nodded his head with a smirk on his face.

"The hard top's yours, and the convertible is for Tina!"

Vanity watched as Lloyd and Tina rushed off to the twin-model Porsches.

"You do know you're spoiling him, right?" she asked.

"That's my Lil' Man!" Boss replied as he dropped his arm around Vanity's shoulders and led her over to the armored Land Rover Range Rover truck he had bought for her.

Boss and Vanity left their high-rise building with Lloyd and Tina following behind them in their new cars. Boss then drove out to Collins Smokehouse, the restaurant at which he was a silent partner. He was also a partner in two gentlemen's clubs and an exotic car dealership. He turned the Land Rover into the already packed parking lot and found a space. As he and Vanity stepped out of the truck, they saw a smiling Lloyd climbing out of his birthday gift.

They all entered the restaurant a few minutes later, to instantly hear the whispering and see people staring at them. Boss ignored it all as he held his arm around Vanity's shoulders and looked around the place.

"ReSean!"

Boss heard his name called and looked over to his right, where he saw Mrs. Collins rushing toward him. He released Vanity just as Evelyn fell into him and wrapped her arms around his waist in a hug.

"ReSean, what are you doing here?" Evelyn Collins questioned as she held her adopted son tightly.

She then leaned back a little to kiss him on his cheek.

"I got here early this morning," Boss answered her. "I'm only going to be here a few hours though. I need to get back to Chicago with my dad!"

"Well, you need to go and say hello to your other father back in the office!" Evelyn told him as she gently pushed him in the direction of the owner's office.

Evelyn watched Boss as he headed to the back of the restaurant. She shook her head and was still smiling when she looked back at Vanity and noticed her new grandson, Lloyd.

"Hey, Lloyd. How's my grandbaby doing?"

"Hi, Grandma!" Lloyd replied, smiling at Boss's adopted mother, who was now his grandmother.

~ ~ ~

Boss popped in on Mr. Collins and saw that he was on the phone. He stood at the door waiting while his adopted father finished up his call.

"ReSean!" Mr. Collins called out with a smile after hanging up the phone. He then stood up, and he and Boss embraced each other. "I thought you was in Chicago with your father?"

"I had to handle a little business here in Miami!" Boss told the older man. "Vanity, Lloyd, and Tina are out front. Lloyd's birthday is tomorrow, so I wanted to do something for him before I headed back to Chicago."

"Let's go see my daughter-in-law and grandson!" Mr.

Collins stated as he and Boss left the office and headed back out front.

Once they were in the dining area, Boss instantly spotted the crowd and recognized Eazy and Erica standing with a few of the guys on the team. Boss and Mr. Collins then walked over to the group.

"What's good, family?" Boss asked as he and Mr. Collins appeared.

"Oh shit!" Eazy yelled out happily after seeing Boss, only to be rewarded with a slap to the arm by Mrs. Collins. "My fault, Mama!"

Evelyn rolled her eyes at her son and then got everyone to sit down at three tables that they pulled together, just as Trigger and Gigi entered the restaurant.

"I knew I recognized the Land Rover outside," Trigger said with a big smile as he and Gigi walked over to the rest of their people.

"Is there anybody else coming?" Evelyn asked while standing with her hands on her hips and staring directly at Boss.

"How do I know?" he replied while trying not to laugh. "I was with Dad in the back."

"Princess and Widow are on their way!" Trigger announced as he and Gigi sat across from Boss and Vanity.

"Rico, Butter, and Magic are on their way too, Mrs. Collins!" one of Eazy and Boss's boys yelled out, only to receive a look from Evelyn and cause all the others to burst out laughing in unison.

~ ~ ~

Malcolm Jr. had gotten word that Boss was back in Miami, so he and his boys headed toward Collins Smokehouse. Malcolm Jr. sat staring out the front passenger window of his G-Wagen as Moses drove. He shifted his eyes to the side mirror and saw the two Escalades driving behind them filled with ten of his men, with five in each truck.

"What's the plan?" Moses asked, after glancing over.

Malcolm Jr. remained quiet a few moments even after hearing Moses's question.

"Just be ready to shoot if shit gets crazy!"

~ ~ ~

After hugging and kissing Mrs. Collins goodbye as he and the others got ready to leave once everyone had finished eating, Boss walked over to where Eazy, Trigger, and the others were standing just outside the restaurant. They were all smoking and talking. Vanity and Gigi left to head to the club, while Lloyd and Tina left to go do their own things.

"What's up, fam?" Eazy said as Boss walked up onto the group. "How long you and these fools plan on being out here?"

"Not much longer!" Boss answered, just as his phone started to ring.

He dug it out of his pocket and saw that his father was calling.

"Yeah, Pops!"

"Everything's set up, Son!"

Boss immediately understood what his father was talking about. He smiled just as he shifted his eyes to see the Benz truck pull up.

"Big Bruh!" Trigger said, tapping Boss on the arm.

Trigger had also peeped the G-Wagen with the two

Escalade trucks behind turning into the parking lot.

"Pops, let me hit you back!" Boss told his father before hanging up.

Boss watched Moses, who he recognized as Malcolm Jr.'s personal bodyguard, climb out of the G-Wagen seconds before the two Escalades emptied out.

"Looks like we about to have some fun!" Trigger stated with a devilish smirk on his lips as he was already sliding his right hand under his shirt.

Boss watched as Malcolm Jr. climbed from the G-Wagen and then walked around the front end of the Benz truck. Boss kept his eyes locked on his so-called brother.

"So, what's up, fam? What we doing?" Eazy spoke up.

Boss heard the question but remained quiet while staring at Malcolm Jr., who stood a few feet away and was staring straight back at him. Boss started toward him, which caused Malcolm Jr.'s men to swing up their weapons, the exact same instant that Trigger and his boys did the same. Boss ignored the guns and walked right up to Malcolm Jr., only for Moses to step in front of his boss.

"First and last warning. Get the fuck out of the way!" Boss told the bodyguard, who flinched just slightly but remained standing where he was.

"Moses!" Malcolm Jr. spoke up, which caused Moses to step aside.

Boss followed Moses with his eyes off to the left of Malcolm Jr. Boss then shifted his eyes slowly back to Malcolm Jr. and met his eyes.

"You showed up here for a reason, but I really don't care what the fuck your reasons are. I tell you what though. I'm not going to say this but one time only. Because of Malcolm and the fact that you're supposed to be my father's son, I'ma fall back from this beef we got. But if I hear at any time that you crossed my family or fucked with my wife, not even Malcolm will keep me from coming to see about you. Do you, and I'ma do me!"

Boss turned his back to Malcolm Jr. and then nodded for his crew to get ready to leave as he started walking toward Trigger's Chevy 1500.

~ ~ ~

Malcolm Jr. was quiet after leaving the soul food restaurant parking lot, after dealing with his supposed younger brother. He sat staring out of his window thinking about not only his feelings concerning what was said by Boss, but also his sudden mixed emotions concerning the sudden closeness between his father and Boss.

After losing his train of thought after hearing his phone ring, Malcolm Jr. dug out his cell phone and saw that Destiny was calling.

"What, Destiny?"

"Where the hell are you, Malcolm? I told you I was stopping by the house before I left!"

"I just left from handling something with your boyfriend."

"My boyfriend? Who? Boss?" Destiny asked. "Where he at?"

"He's in Miami, Destiny! I just met the nigga at Collins Smokehouse," Malcolm Jr. told his step-sister.

After complete silence for a few moments, he looked at the phone's screen to see that Destiny had already hung up on him.

Malcolm Jr. shook his head as he dropped the phone into his lap. He laughed lightly thinking about how everybody seemed to just be drawn to this nigga Boss for some reason.

3

Boss got a look at Club Empire now that the place was finished and scheduled to open that Friday. He then spent the rest of what time he had with Vanity, even allowing her to drag him back to the penthouse where she basically raped him. Of course, he had to admit that he enjoyed every minute of it.

Vanity drove out along with Boss to the airstrip once it was time for him to head back to Chicago. He sat in the back seat of the Land Rover Range Rover with Vanity while Princess drove.

"How long exactly do you plan on being in Chicago, Boss?" she asked as she lay against him while he ran his hand through her hair, which was a habit he seemed to have.

"Ma, I can't answer that right now!" Boss admitted. "I'm helping my pops deal with some problems up there, and I'm also trying to make sure business on our end is set up in Chicago as well."

Boss heard Vanity sucking her teeth and saw the way her face balled up. She lifted her head from his chest and met his eyes.

"I understand what you're doing, but you can't forget that you have a woman and son back here waiting for you. Just promise me that you'll hurry up and get back home, Boss."

"You got that, ma!" Boss promised before kissing Vanity's soft lips.

Once they arrived at the airstrip and said their goodbyes, Boss, Trigger, and Black Widow boarded the private jet. Boss looked out of his seat window and saw Vanity standing with Gigi and Princess but staring directly at him. He winked his eye at her, which caused her to crack a small smile and wave to him.

~ ~ ~

As soon as Boss's jet landed in Chicago from Miami, he walked over to his Bentley which was waiting for him with Savage in the driver's seat.

"What's good, Big Homie?" Boss said in greeting to Savage.

"What it do, Boss!" Savage replied as the two touched fists.

"Everything, everything!" Boss replied as he climbed

into the back of the Bentley with Trigger holding open the door while Black Widow climbed in behind him.

Once they were inside the car and Savage was driving away from the airstrip, Boss called his father's phone.

"Hello!"

"Pops, it's Boss. I'm back!"

"Good! I'm going to need you to come to the Holiday Inn down the street from the penthouse you're staying at."

"Everything good?"

"Yeah. I just want to talk to you about something."

"All right, Pops. I'ma be there after I check on business."

After hanging up with his father, Boss then went to check in with Rachell. He sat and listened to the line until it was answered on the third ring.

"Hello!"

Boss was confused when the person answering the phone was not Rachell.

"Who is this?"

"Demi! Who am I speaking with?"

"Can you let Mrs. Harris know that Boss is on the phone?"

Boss waited for a response but only received silence. He

was just about to call out to Demi, when she finally spoke up.

"Umm, Boss. This is Demi Harris. My mother is kind of in a meeting right now with a Mr. Hernandez."

"Seven Hernandez?" Boss asked, with his face all balled up.

"I think so. Would you like me—?"

"Let Rachell know I called as soon as she's free!" Boss told Demi before hanging up the phone right afterward.

"What's up, Boss?" Savage answered when he looked back at Boss through the rear-view mirror.

"Change of plans, Big Homie!" Boss told him, which caused Trigger to turn his head back and look at him.

Boss then began to explain to Trigger what he wanted him to do and what they might end up doing together.

~ ~ ~

"I expect to hear from you within a few hours, Rachell!" Seven Hernandez told her as he was stepping out of her front door once their discussion was finished.

Rachell stared daggers at Hernandez as the son of a bitch walked out to his Rolls-Royce along with his bodyguards. She slammed her front door behind him and then turned and started straight toward her office to make a phone call.

"Mom!"

Rachell stopped and looked back behind her to see her daughter walking toward her.

"Yes, Demi? What is it?"

"You okay?" Demi asked her mother, seeing the look on her face.

"I'm fine, honey!" Rachell told her daughter with a dismissive wave of her hand. "What was it you wanted, Demi? I've got an important phone call I have to make."

"I just wanted to tell you that while you were in your meeting, you had a phone call."

"Who was it?"

"Boss!" Demi answered with a small smile. "He wants you to call him after you are done with your meeting."

"Damn it!" Rachell said as she rushed off and headed to her home office.

She snatched up her cell phone as soon as she reached her desk, and quickly called Boss's phone.

"Yeah!"

"Boss, where are you?"

"Why?"

"Boss, listen!" Rachell said breathlessly as she explained about Seven Hernandez and his unexpected drop-in visit at her home as well as the threats he made if she wasn't going to agree to his demands.

"Relax, Rachell!" Boss calmly replied. "I gave you my word that I would deal with him, right?"

"Of course!"

"Watch the news!"

Rachell heard Boss hang up the phone after his comment. She then stared at her phone and then stared at her office wall in deep thought.

"Mom!"

Rachell lost her train of thought and looked over at her office door to see her daughter standing there watching her.

"Yes, honey?" Rachell asked, setting down her phone.

"Are you okay?"

Rachell nodded her head yes in response to Demi's question. She then pointed to the wall-unit flat-screen that was directly across from the desk.

"Sweetheart, turn on the television and bring me the remote, please."

~ ~ ~

"So, what's up, big Bruh?" Trigger asked, looking into the back seat at Boss once he had hung up on the phone.

Boss heard his baby brother but didn't respond right away. Instead, he called up front to Savage.

"What's up, Boss?" Savage questioned, lifting his eyes from the road a moment to meet Boss's eyes in the rear-view mirror.

"Next time the Rolls-Royce stops, pull up beside it!" Boss informed Savage as he pulled his Ruger from his right shoulder holster.

Trigger slowly smiled when realizing that his big brother was about to put in some work. He then chuckled at what he was going to witness.

Five minutes later the Rolls-Royce slowed to a stop at a red light. Boss waited until Savage stopped the Bentley beside the car, and then he calmly opened his back door and climbed out, with his Ruger in his right hand down at his side.

Boss walked straight up to the back door of the Rolls and smirked when it opened right up.

"What the—!"

Boom! Boom! Boom! Boom!

Brrrr! Brrrr! Brrrr!

Boss slowly turned his head to his left after completely erasing Seven Hernandez's face. He then saw the driver's window to the Rolls-Royce blown out and the driver hanging out dead. Boss looked back into the car at Hernandez for a moment before turning and stepping back over to his Bentley, just as Trigger was letting his window up front back up.

~ ~ ~

"Mom!" Demi called out as she and Rachell sat watching the news in of her mother's office.

Rachell listened to her daughter but didn't respond while she sat and continued to watch the news changing from story to story. She then paused as breaking news interrupted. She sat forward as she set down the remote after turning up the volume.

Rachell continued to focus her full attention on the news broadcast. She sat up in her seat when she heard Seven Hernandez's name. She continued to watch as the reporter announced that he and his two bodyguards were murdered while sitting at the traffic light.

"Mom!" Demi said while listening to the news report.

"Isn't that the same Seven Hernandez that just left here a few minutes ago?"

Rachell heard her phone begin ringing before she could answer her daughter's question. Rachell then looked down at her cell phone and smiled a little bit when she saw who was on the other line.

"Hello, Boss!" Rachell said, after answering the call.

"Are you watching the news?"

"I am!"

"So you see your problem?"

"I see it, Boss!"

"We'll speak later, Rachell!"

Rachell smiled a little harder after Boss hung up the phone. She then shook her head as she set her phone back down.

"Mom, what happened?" Demi asked.

"He's amazing!" Rachell replied while still smiling. "He is truly amazing!"

4

Three days after Boss, Trigger, and Black Widow returned to Chicago, Eazy was back to handling business and making sure everything was running smoothly. Any small problems were dealt with immediately.

On the Friday night of the grand opening of Vanity and Gigi's Club Empire, Eazy got the whole crew together in Miami to show up to support the girls.

"Oh my God!" Erica cried in shock and disbelief once Eazy turned his new Mercedes-Benz S550 down the street on which the club was located.

There was an unbelievably long line of cars and SUVs all trying to get a parking spot at the club.

"Eazy, do you see this, babe?" Erica said.

"Hell yeah!" Eazy answered as he was driving behind a trail of cars.

Once he was up front, he pulled in front of a dark-colored Escalade truck. Eazy then lowered his window at the front entrance where armed security guards stood, which were hired by Vanity for safety.

"Eazy, what's up, man?" the guard called out, remembering Eazy after being introduced to him once he was hired for the job.

"What up, main man?" Eazy responded.

He conversed with the guard for a brief moment and found out that Butter and the others were already inside.

Eazy pulled into the parking lot and parked in a spot that was saved for him by Vanity. He shut off the Benz, and then both he and Erica got out and started walking toward the front entrance.

"Eazy, do you see this crowd?" Erica said, shaking her head at the huge sea of people everywhere.

They got into the club with no problems at all since the doorman knew who he and Erica were. Eazy led his lady into the club, only to get hit by the bass from the club's speakers. Rick Ross and Trey Songz's "This is the Life!" was banging from the speakers.

"Oh my God!" Erica screamed again, grabbing onto Eazy's arm once she and Eazy got further inside the club. They saw the huge stage, and she couldn't believe her eyes when she saw both Rick Ross and Trey Songz performing live.

Eazy looked over at Erica and smiled at how excited she was since he knew how much she loved Trey Songz. He shook his head as he draped his arm around her shoulders, and they began making their way into the VIP section.

They took the steps to the upstairs-level club and walked past security, where they saw their crew. Eazy yelled to his people to get their attention.

"About time y'all got here!" Rico yelled over the music as he and Eazy embraced each other. "What took you guys so long?"

"Waiting on Erica!" Eazy answered with a roll of his eyes as he showed and received love from the rest of the crew and his boys' dates or their main ladies. "Hey, where are Vanity and Gigi?"

"They left about ten minutes ago to handle something," Magic yelled as he handed Eazy a bottle of Ace of Spades.

~ ~ ~

Vanity was dealing with a small problem with the girls back in the locker room and then found her girl and business partner, Gigi, inside her office next door. She stood at Gigi's door a few moments watching her girl standing in the middle of the office talking on her cell phone, and catching

Trigger's name. Vanity just shook her head, smiled, and then cleared her throat, causing Gigi to spin around to face her.

Vanity listened as Gigi told Trigger that she needed to go.

"Girl, what does Trigger's ass want now?" Vanity asked as Gigi lowered her phone from her ear.

"I called him!" Gigi admitted. "I miss my man!"

Vanity laughed as she walked into the office past Gigi and sat down on the corner of her desk.

"I am not going to comment, but I did just see Eazy and Eric walk in."

"Did you handle Passion and Diamond's little problem?" Gigi asked, just as there was a knock on the door.

"Yeah, Princess!" Vanity said when she looked up and saw her at the office door.

"We've got visitors!" Princess informed Vanity. "Malcolm Jr. and his people just walked into the club."

Vanity sighed as she shook her head, since she was really not in the mood to deal with Malcolm Jr. and his bullshit. She pushed off of Gigi's desk and walked out of the office with Princess and Gigi right behind her.

Once she got back out onto the main floor with a team of

security and her girls, Vanity instantly spotted Malcolm Jr. and his people. She walked through the crowd and headed directly toward them.

"What are you doing here, Malcolm?" Vanity yelled over the music as she and her team stopped in front of him and his people.

"I'm impressed!" Malcolm Jr. said, looking around and slowly nodding his head. "This place really looks good in here."

"Again!" Vanity restated. "What are you doing here?"

"Am I not welcomed?" Malcolm Jr. inquired, finally looking at Vanity and meeting her eyes. "I'm here to show my support and have a good time."

"Well, I think—!" Vanity began, but stopped as she first felt Gigi nudge her and then looked over to where her girl was nodding.

She instantly spotted Eazy and the whole crew pushing through the crowd and heading straight toward them.

"Vanity, what's up?" Eazy asked as he and the crew stopped beside her but stared directly at Malcolm Jr. "We got a problem?"

Vanity stared at Malcolm Jr., who paid no attention to

Eazy.

"Everything is fine, Eazy. Malcolm is just here to show his support and to enjoy his night. He's fine!" Vanity informed him.

Malcolm Jr. slowly smiled and finally shifted his eyes from Vanity over toward Eazy. He gave a light laugh and walked off with his crew, leaving Eazy and the others simply staring at him.

Vanity shook her head and sighed, hoping tonight's opening would continue to be a great success.

~ ~ ~

After the problem with Seven Hernandez was handled and everything had cooled down, Boss went about conducting business with his father and Rachell. He got in contact with new buyers in both Miami and Atlanta, and he also found himself in three different meetings in which he spoke with Josophe Nelson and Armando Price. He then spoke with Perry St. Thomas, who was interested in learning about the plans of being a part of the Warren and Harris collaboration. St. Thomas was known for selling the same products as the collaboration.

"Well, I tell you what!" Boss stated as he sat across from

Mr. St. Thomas at the glass table in Rachell's office. "You may have the same products as my father and Ms. Harris, but do you have what I'm also offering?"

"And what exactly are you offering, young Warren?" St. Thomas asked, sitting back in his seat with a questioning expression on his face.

"They're called Blue Devils!" Boss answered as he slowly began to smile when he saw St. Thomas's expression begin to change. "I'm willing to deal in business with you, but there will be a split in business!"

"Wait a minute!" St. Thomas said, holding up his hand for Boss to wait before they went any further. "What are these Blue Devils, and why would I want to have any business with a drug that I've never heard of before?"

Boss slowly smiled at the drug lord's concerns as he sat across from him. He then dug out his cell and made a quick call. Boss spoke on the phone for a few minutes before he hung up and looked back over at St. Thomas.

"Now we wait!"

"Wait for what?" St. Thomas questioned, just as Rachell and Malcolm Sr. stepped into the office.

St. Thomas sat watching as Boss stood up and walked

over to his father and Rachell and began speaking in a lowered voice.

"So, what's the news?" Malcolm Sr. asked in a lowered voice. "What's St. Thomas talking about?"

"Exactly what the both of you said he would say is what he said!" Boss admitted to his father and Rachell. "But I may have a plan though."

"Well, explain!" Malcolm Sr. spoke up, right before he noticed a smile appear on Rachell's face.

Boss then clarified to his father and Rachell about the offer he was planning to make to St. Thomas once he witnessed the effects of the Blue Devils.

"You really think St. Thomas is going to deal with us at the same time, Boss?" Rachell asked with a bit of concern.

"Trust me!" Boss said, winking his eye at Rachell, just as there was a knock on the office door.

"Yes, Bruce!" Rachell called out once the office door was opened and she saw her bodyguard.

"Boss has company!" Bruce announced as he stepped back and allowed Trigger to escort a young, white man inside.

"Who's this?" Malcolm asked, looking from the white

man over to Boss.

Boss did not immediately answer his father; instead, he turned his attention to Trigger, who walked up beside him and whispered into his ear. Boss nodded his head and then accepted the pill that Trigger had dropped into his hand. He then looked back over at the white man.

"Tim, correct?" Boss asked.

After receiving a nod from the man, Boss motioned him over to the table where St. Thomas was still seated and staring up at him and Tim.

"Mr. St. Thomas!" Boss called out in his normal, relaxed voice. "You asked what Blue Devils were and why you would consider dealing with me. Well, to answer your question, this is a Blue Devil!"

St. Thomas stared at the pill that was set down on the table in front of him, and then looked back at Boss.

"This is Tim, Mr. St. Thomas. He is going to show you why you should consider my business offer."

~ ~ ~

"That was unbelievable!" Rachell said, still in shock after witnessing the effects of Boss's Blue Devils soon after the young man had swallowed it.

She wondered what was inside the pill that made it so potent, when she then noticed St. Thomas and Boss shake hands.

"I'll be in contact!" St. Thomas said as Boss escorted him toward the door.

St. Thomas then shook hands with both Malcolm Sr. and Rachell before he exited the office.

Once the office door shut behind St. Thomas, Boss looked at his father and Rachell, only to find them staring at him.

"What?" Boss asked.

"You are amazing!" Rachell replied with a smile. "What was that pill you gave that man, Boss?"

"It's called a Blue Devil," he explained to her, with a small smile appearing on his lips.

"Boss!" Malcolm said, getting his son's attention. "What's inside the capsule?"

Boss slowly smiled as he told both his father and Rachell the ingredients of the Blue Devils. Boss then saw the look they shot one another

"Again, people. This is business, and I'm all about more!"

Malcolm shook his head and smiled at his son, just as his cell phone began to ring. He dug out his phone and saw Brenda was calling.

"Hello!"

"Malcolm, it's Brenda!"

"I'm aware of that, beautiful! What's up?"

Malcolm Sr. listened to Brenda explain to him about the problem she was beginning to have with her soon-to-be ex-husband after she announced she wanted a divorce. Malcolm stood outside in front of Boss's Bentley Flying Spur.

"All right, listen!" Malcolm Sr. told Brenda as he explained to her what he wanted her to do, before he finally hung up on the phone.

"So you're bringing my mom out here?" Boss interrupted.

"Yeah!" Malcolm answered as he held his son's eyes for a moment. "I'm going to deal with Patricia today!"

5

Vanity got through the grand opening of the club and was happy with how the night went, even with her man's older brother and his crew there. She spent the next few days traveling back and forth to each of the clubs, leaving Gigi at Club Empire while she drove back out to her first place. She left Lloyd and Tina with Tina's mother while she was gone, only to end up staying at the townhouse two extra days. She would have stayed a third night had Gigi not called and complained on her voice mail about someone coming by the club.

Vanity called Gigi back and listened to the line ring as she waited until Princess finished her phone call. She then heard Gigi answer the phone.

"Hello!"

"Gigi, it's Vanity. What's this I heard you saying after leaving a message about somebody coming by the club?"

"Vanity, do you know somebody named Steven Wallace?"

"No! Why?"

"Because he's saying that we've got two weeks to be out of the building, that's why!"

"Out of what building, Gigi?"

"Bitch, what building we just started a new club inside of?" Gigi replied sarcastically. "This Wallace guy is supposed to come back by in two weeks, Vanity!"

"Did he leave a number?" Vanity asked her before she quickly grabbed a pen and piece of paper.

She then wrote down the number Gigi had repeated to her.

After hanging up with Gigi after getting Wallace's number, she was just about to call him, when Princess showed up.

"Vanity, we need to get back to Miami, and you need to contact Boss!" Princess informed her. "It's about Malcolm Jr."

"Wait, what about Malcolm Jr., Princess?" Vanity asked, balling up her face in utter confusion.

"Malcolm's been shot and is at the hospital!" Prince informed Vanity, watching her mouth drop open in disbelief.

Vanity and Princess quickly got their things together and jumped into the Land Rover and headed to Miami. Vanity immediately got on the phone to call Boss to let him know what was going on.

"Damn it!" Vanity said, after getting his voice message.

She then remembered the time difference, but she still tried calling him again, only to get his voice mail again.

"Shit!"

"What happened?" Princess questioned, looking over at Vanity and seeing her face all balled up.

"Boss isn't answering the damn phone!" Vanity told Princess while trying to call him again and again.

Once Princess reached the hospital at which she was told Malcolm had been admitted, Vanity was out of the SUV as soon as Princess parked the Land Rover. They rushed inside and right up to the front desk. Vanity started to demand what floor he was on, only for Princess to interrupt and let her know that he was on the fifth floor.

Princess and Vanity took the elevator up and ran off the floor as soon as the door opened. They made their way to the nurses' station on the floor; however, they both stopped when they heard Vanity's name called out.

"What the hell are you doing here?" Vanity asked as she stared nastily at Destiny, who was walking toward them.

"Relax, Vanity!" Princess spoke up, causing Vanity to swing around and look at her. "She's the one who called and told me about Malcolm."

"How the hell do you two—? Oh, never mind that right now," Vanity continued, waving her hand dismissively at the whole subject before she directed another question back toward Destiny. "Where's Malcolm at?"

"He's just been moved into a private room," Destiny explained. "I just went to get something to eat, but Malcolm's asleep now. You can see him if you want to."

Vanity and Princess allowed Destiny to lead the way to Malcolm's hospital room. They walked inside and were shocked to see him in the bed with tubes running everywhere.

"Oh my God!" Vanity cried out, quickly rushing over to his bedside and looking down at him.

"What happened?" Princess asked, looking over at Destiny.

"I'm not really sure!" Destiny answered, shaking her head sadly. "I just got a call right as I was getting ready to leave to fly back to Chicago. I'm not sure who the caller was, but he told me about Malcolm; and when I found him, he was inside his car slumped over the steering wheel. He took three bullets to the chest, and two hit him in the left shoulder."

"Where's Moses?" Vanity asked while looking over at Destiny. "Isn't Moses his bodyguard?"

"That's just it, Vanity. Malcolm let Moses go, since he was getting out!" she explained to her.

"Getting out of what?" Princess asked, staring oddly at Vanity.

Destiny shook her head and then began to explain herself.

"What you all don't know about Malcolm that he didn't let most people see was that he already felt like he wasn't worth much since Malcolm Sr. treated him as if he really wasn't his son or even important to him. And since Boss showed up and he saw how Malcolm Sr. took to him so easily, Malcolm Jr. felt that he would just leave the family business. He said that Malcolm Sr. finally got the son that he always wanted."

"So Malcolm was leaving the family business because of Boss and Malcolm Sr.'s relationship? Is that what you're telling us?" Vanity inquired, looking from Destiny back to

>**J.L. ROSE**

Malcolm Jr., and now looking at him in a different light.

~ ~ ~

Vanity stayed with Malcolm until he finally woke up for a few moments. She couldn't get him to speak; however, she received a small smile in return from him before his eyes shut and he fell back asleep. Vanity was still with him when Moses finally showed up. She allowed the bodyguard to have some time with his friend, but she noticed the anger on his face before she left the room.

She dug out her phone once she stepped into the hallway and called Boss's number again. But just like before she only got his voice mail.

"Vanity!"

She looked behind her and saw Princess walking up the hallway toward her as she put her phone down.

"What's up, Princess?"

"We've got a problem!" Princess informed her. "Eazy just called me. There have been some problems with some crew members who just showed up, but no one knows who's the head of the crew."

"Has Eazy called Boss yet?"

"He's out in the city with Butter and Rico right now.

>56

From what he told me, there was a shoot-out after the spot almost got robbed!"

Vanity shook her head thinking about how Boss would react once he found out about what was going on. She tried calling her man once more.

"Hello!" Boss sleepily answered after three rings.

"Shit!" Vanity mumbled, after hearing Boss's voice and realizing that she was stuck with not only telling him about his brother being in the hospital but also about the bullshit that was going on.

~ ~ ~

Boss got out of bed and dressed after hanging up with Vanity. He then called Trigger and had him get with the rest of the team and explain that they were leaving and heading back to Miami again. He then called his father's number.

"Hello!" Malcolm Sr. answered half asleep after two rings.

"Pops, it's Boss! We've got a problem!"

"What's the problem, Son?" Malcolm Sr. asked, after sighing loudly into the phone.

Boss explained to his father about the first problem concerning his business and then about the problem with his

and Vanity's new Club Empire. He left the new news about
Malcolm Jr. for last, and Boss wasn't surprised at all when
his father yelled excitedly after hearing about his son.

He continued getting himself together while trying to get
his father to calm down. Boss then explained that he would
handle things in Miami, and he then further explained that
he was leaving everything for him and Rachell to take care
of business-wise until he got back to Chicago.

After hanging up with his father and turning around to
head out of his bedroom to leave, he saw Trigger was already
standing in the doorway. Boss then tossed him a Louis
Vuitton duffel bag.

"Let's go remind Miami who's the king of the city!"
Boss told Trigger as he led the way out of the bedroom.

~ ~ ~

Steven Wallace walked into the bathroom of the
penthouse suite at which he was staying for the time being.
But he paused at the bathroom door and stared at the
extremely gorgeous woman who stood inside the shower.
Steven was so caught up in staring at her curves through the
glass that he never noticed she was watching him.

"You plan on standing there staring, or are you going to

join me in here?" Brandi asked from inside the shower.

Steven smiled at Brandi's invitation and began undressing until he was fully naked. He then climbed into the shower with Brandi, dropping his eyes down to her rounded and firm but soft ass.

She shook her head when she saw the stupid look on his face, but she needed his dumb ass to finish out the plans that she already had in motion. But she also needed something hard and stiff inside of her, so she turned and faced him.

"Are you going to stand there, or are you going to take what you want? Or do I have to take control?"

Brandi didn't want Steven to respond. She reached out and grabbed him by the back of the neck, pushed him down onto his knees, and then pulled his face into her overheated and wet womanhood. She shut her eyes and moaned once his tongue went to work licking her wet box.

Brandi forced him to eat her pussy until she climaxed all over his face and inside his mouth. She then pushed him away once she got control of herself and looked down at him as he sat on the shower floor.

"Get up and fuck me!"

Brandi took full control even though Steven was doing

most of the work behind her as he slammed his it-will-do-for-now penis inside of her from the back. She had to reach back with her right hand and spread her ass cheeks so he could get deeper inside. She concentrated on thoughts of Boss and began playing with her clit.

Brandi almost lost focus when Steven cried out like a female announcing that he was just about to cum, so she quickly got herself off cumming all over his dick. But before he could cum inside her, she backed away from him. Before he could begin crying and complaining about not cumming, she finished him off with a firm hand job. But just as he began cumming, she released his dick and climbed out of the shower, leaving his ass in the shower whimpering like a little bitch.

~ ~ ~

About fifteen minutes after Steven had gotten out of the shower and made a quick phone call, Brandi was already in the bed watching the television when he finally joined her under the covers.

"You okay, baby?" he asked as he reached over and pulled Brandi over into his arms, not seeing the rolling of her eyes as she moved over to lie beside him.

"I'm not going to be fine until you keep your promise, Steven!" Brandi told him as she sat up to look down into his face. "I've told you what these people here in Miami have done to me, and you promised to help me get them back. You said you loved me, so I expect you to keep your word, Steven!"

"Did I not already step to this bitch who works for or with Vanity?" Steven asked her. "I've already made it known that I'm taking over that club in two weeks, so just relax and let me handle this!"

"Steven, was you not listening to me, nigga?" Brandi yelled with a lot of attitude.

Brandi then stared down at him like he was even more stupid than she already thought he was.

"Nigga, two days is too muthafucking long! I give it two days, or maybe one, and this crazy-ass fool Boss will be back in Miami. Are you fucking listening?"

"Fuck is you tripping about?" Steven screamed as he started to get upset seeing the way Brandi was acting at the mention of whoever the nigga Boss was. "Fuck this pussy muthafucka! He got guns. I got 'em too. He got killers, and I fucking got 'em too!"

"But you don't got—!"

"Fuck all that!" Steven yelled as he threw the blanket off of him and climbed out of the bed. But before he left the bedroom, he turned around, looked back at Brandi, and said, "I don't know who you think I am, but I'm on this gangsta shit just like the next nigga is, and once this shit's over, you gonna learn to respect me!"

"You probably won't even be breathing once this is all over, because you won't listen to what I'm telling your ass!" Brandi said to herself as she sat shaking her head after he stormed from the bedroom.

6

Once Boss arrived back in Miami on Malcolm Sr.'s private jet, he was greeted by Eazy and the rest of the crew, who were all waiting for him at the airstrip. Boss led Trigger, Savage, Black Widow, and Joker over to the new Benz that Eazy was leaning up against.

"Welcome the fuck back!" Eazy stated as he embraced Boss.

Boss then hugged Butter, Rico, and Magic.

"So what's really the problem out here?" Boss asked as he looked back toward his main man.

"Truthfully, my dude," Eazy started as he shook his head, "I really ain't sure what the fuck is going on! One moment shit is going good, and then out of nowhere two spots get hit, and we going to war with muthafuckas we don't even know!"

"What all we lose?" Boss asked him.

"A few soldiers!" Rico answered.

"We got to the spot before we lost any work or money though!" Magic added.

"Let's go!" Boss ordered as he opened the passenger door to the Benz and climbed inside.

Trigger got in the back seat with him while the others walked over and stepped into the Escalade Premium Butter was driving.

Once they were inside, Boss questioned Eazy about what was going on with the visit Vanity had received at the club.

"From what Princess told me, Bruh, it's some clown-ass nigga named Steven Wallace. What's crazy is that the dude even left a number to get back at him with!"

"I'ma deal with that!" Boss stated as he dug out his phone from his pocket, just as Eazy spoke up again.

"You hear about ya brother?"

Boss heard Eazy's question but didn't bother to reply as he sat listening to the line ring while calling Vanity. Boss caught the way Eazy looked at him, and shook his head.

"Hello!" Vanity answered at the start of the third ring.

"Where you at, Vanity?" Boss asked while taking the blunt Eazy had just handed to him.

Vanity remained quiet for a few moments.

"Boss, where are you? Are you still in Chicago?"

"I'm back in Miami, ma! I'm in the car with Eazy now,"

Boss explained before he again asked where she was.

"I'm at the hospital, Boss!"

"The what?" he yelled.

"Boss, relax!" Vanity quickly interrupted him, hearing the instant anger in his voice. "I'm with Malcolm Jr. at the hospital, Boss."

"Fuck is you doing!"

"Boss!" Vanity yelled, cutting him off. "That's enough of all this lil' boy bullshit you and Malcolm are on. This is your damn brother laid up in this hospital bed after being shot up and almost dying. You need to get your ass over here, act like a man, and see about your brother!"

Boss heard Vanity hang up the phone after going off on him. He then lowered the phone from his ear.

"Yo, E! We going out to Parkway Hospital, fam!"

~ ~ ~

Vanity lowered her cell phone from her ear after just going off on Boss. She surprised herself since that wasn't really her nature. She shut her eyes and sighed deeply.

"Was you just defending me, gorgeous?" she heard a voice ask.

Vanity quickly opened her eyes and looked over at

Malcolm Jr., only to see him staring back at her. She got up from her seat beside his bed to stand.

"How do you feel?"

"Pain!" Malcolm said. "Can I at least get some water, please?"

Vanity walked into the bathroom and got him a glass of water. Once he had finished, she asked him if he wanted any more.

"Naw!" he replied sounding a bit stronger. "I'm good!"

"What happened, Malcolm? Who shot you?" Vanity asked after she set the cup on the table next to the bed.

Malcolm shook his head slowly while trying to remember.

"I didn't really see his face. He crept up onto my blind side."

"You sure it was a he?"

"Yeah! I know it was a light-skinned guy, but I can't remember his face!"

"You remember what he had on?"

Malcolm shook his head again, still trying to remember.

"I just remember some tattoo he had on his neck."

"What type of tattoo?"

"I can't remember really."

"Remember what?" both Vanity and Malcolm Jr. heard a voice call out from behind them.

They both turned around and looked at the hospital room door and saw Boss step inside, with both Trigger and Eazy right behind him.

"Am I interrupting?" Boss asked as he walked up beside Vanity and accepted a hug and kiss while never looking over at Malcolm Jr.

"Thank you for coming!" Vanity whispered into Boss's ear before releasing him.

She then looked at Malcolm and then back at Boss.

"Malcolm was just telling me about what he could remember about who shot him!" Vanity said aloud.

"Oh really?" Boss stated while still staring at Vanity.

When Vanity saw Boss's facial expression and picked up on his attitude, she shot him a nasty look.

"Eazy! Trigger! You two boys walk me to get something to eat and let Boss talk to his brother!"

Boss watched as both his boys walked out of the room with Vanity. He then heard Malcolm speak up as soon as the room door shut behind them.

"ReSean, look—!"

"It's Boss, playboy!" Boss reminded him, shooting Malcolm Jr. a look after interrupting him.

"All right then, Boss!" Malcolm replied with a slight smile. "I understand that you hate me and—!"

"I don't hate you!" Boss interrupted him again. "To hate means I would have some type of feelings toward you, and I don't even know you, dude. I just know we supposed to have the same father."

Malcolm nodded his head.

"All right! I'll just say this and let you do you since you really ain't trying to hear shit I gotta say. I'm—I'm sorry about everything we had going on. Everything I did and tried to do to you. I guess I was just jealous and envied the fact that since I was young I tried everything to get Malcolm to notice that I was worth more than what people had him believing I would be. It's hard trying to live up to what your father was; but to see you come and easily become accepted, I understood my place. And just so you know, Boss, I'm leaving the city, and it's yours, little brother. I won't be in your way anymore."

~ ~ ~

Vanity stood outside Malcolm's room talking with Eazy and the others, who filled her in on everything that was going on. She and the others looked at the door when they heard it open and saw Boss walk out of the room. She stared at her man's face but could see nothing that would tell her about his mood.

"Where's Moses?" Boss asked while looking over at Vanity.

"Moses left after Malcolm had security make him leave!" Vanity explained to him. "He's close by though. He's called twice to let me know that he wasn't far away if I needed him for anything."

Boss nodded his head and then looked at Rico.

"Rico, get two of our best shooters out here. I want them posted out in front of this door. I don't give a fuck who it is, but nobody but Vanity or me had better get into that room! Are we clear?" Boss ordered.

"I got you, Boss!" Rico replied as he quickly picked up his phone and stepped away from the group.

Boss then looked over at Eazy.

"E, you already know what's next, fam! Game time's over with, playboy! It's murder season, so make sure these niggas we got on the team ready to put in work. Because as soon as we find out who's behind this bullshit, it's time to paint the streets red!"

"That's what I been waiting to fucking hear!" Trigger jumped in, smiling an evil-looking grin while rubbing his hands together.

"Black! Princess!" Boss called out, looking at both his female killers. "I'ma need both of you to hold shit down with Vanity and Gigi until I find out who this Steven Wallace clown is."

"We got it, pretty boy!" Princess replied with a smile.

Boss was interrupted by his ringing phone before he could finish, so he dug it out of his pocket and answered without checking the caller ID.

"Who's this?"

"You in Miami?"

Boss recognized his father's voice and stepped away from his crew.

"What's up, Pops?"

"How's Malcolm?"

"He'll make it!" Boss replied. "Pops, tell me something. Did you know Malcolm almost died while he was trying to leave the city because he felt you wanted me to run the city?"

"What?"

Boss provided his father with the short version of what Malcolm Jr. had expressed to him.

"I'ma do what I can to get this shit right out here, but afterward, you need to talk to Malcolm because it's a misunderstanding, I'm hoping. Because I'm not looking for a handout from nobody. My brother was out here holding shit down before I came into the picture. So if I'm right, then you need to clear shit up with your son!"

"Damn!" Malcolm Sr. stated with a little laugh. "I thought I was the father; but I hear what you're saying, and I'll clear up this misunderstanding, Son!"

"Thanks!"

"One more thing!" Malcolm told Boss. "I've got two messages for you."

"I'm listening."

"One's from your mother. She's here, and she wants you to be careful and get back to Chicago."

"What's the second message, Pops?"

"We've got men flying out there to assist you," Malcolm Sr. informed his son. "St. Thomas sent fifteen of his men to

Miami, and Rachell sent ten men along with the fifteen I also sent to assist you. You know Cole, who's my second behind Ike. Finally, Rachell also sent Louis, and St. Thomas sent Jones."

Boss nodded his head, even though his father couldn't see him.

"Tell mom I said I'll see her soon!" Boss told his father.

After hanging up with his father, Boss sighed aloud and deeply as he turned around to see Vanity standing only a few feet away, leaning up against the wall with her arms folded across her chest, watching him. He walked over to her and grabbed her around her small waist as she reached up and wrapped her arms around his neck.

"Thank you," Vanity told him while smiling up at Boss.

"Thank you for what?" Boss responded with a confused look on his face.

"For being the man I knew you was, and the man I fell in love with, Boss!" Vanity explained. "I heard what you told your father about your brother, and I'm happy to see that you're willing to do the right thing, babe."

~ ~ ~

Boss received a call back from Detective Aaron Wright,

who let him know that he was outside. Boss told Vanity and the others he would be back, and then rode the elevator downstairs. He walked out of the hospital to see a smoke-gray Jaguar XKR coupe that was slowly pulling to a stop in front of the hospital.

"Let's go for a ride!" Detective Wright called out from inside his Jaguar.

Boss walked out to the car, opened up the passenger door, and climbed inside. He caught a quick glimpse of Trigger exiting the hospital and staring straight at him. He then shut the car door once he was inside.

Once the detective drove off from the hospital parking lot, Boss watched as he produced a brown folder, that he tossed over to him.

"That's what I found on this Steven Wallace guy you asked about," Detective Wright told Boss, glancing over at him.

Boss opened the file and read what was in front of him, and saw that Wallace was twenty-eight years old and from Orlando. He continued reading and noticed that homeboy had a few arrests and was making a little money.

"What got this dude out here in Miami, Cop? How's he

even know me?"

"I've got somebody on that now!" Detective Wright informed Boss. "I'm trying to find out where he's laid out at. I'm going to put a tail on him to find out what I can, and then I'll let you know."

"You do that!" Boss told the detective before he said, "Pull over!"

Once the detective did as he was told, Boss told him to call him as soon as he knew something. Boss then climbed out of the Jaguar with the file in hand and walked back to the Escalade that had been tailing them.

Boss climbed inside the Escalade and shut the door behind him as Trigger pulled off. Boss then sat back and sighed tiredly.

"What's the cop got for you?" Trigger asked, glancing over toward Boss.

"Seems like we've got some foreigner out here trying to make some noise," Boss told Trigger.

He then continued to explain what he knew so far, and even began reading from the file that Detective Wright had given to him.

7

After being back in Miami for two weeks, Vanity noticed how quiet the streets were all of a sudden since her man was now seen all over the city making it known that the king was home again. But for some reason, Vanity still felt something was cooking up and was about to happen no matter how many times Boss told her to relax and that he had everything under control.

Vanity woke up on Friday morning to the news that Boss was leaving town for a while, which worried her a little since the warning she had received from Steven Wallace was in two weeks.

"Relax, ma!" was all she received in return from Boss.

Vanity tried to relax after Boss and Trigger left for the airstrip to supposedly fly back to Chicago. They even took Lloyd and Tina with them. Vanity then met up with Gigi at the apartment she had out in Aventura.

"Hey, girl!" Gigi stated after opening her front door to see Vanity and Princess standing there.

"You still not ready?" Vanity asked as she entered the

apartment and saw Black Widow leaving Gigi's kitchen with a sub sandwich.

Gigi closed and locked the door behind Princess as she walked back to the den. There she found Vanity, the twin sisters, and their personal bodyguard already sitting down.

"So, Vanity, is it true?"

"Is what true?" Vanity asked, looking from Black Widow over toward Gigi. "What are you talking about?"

"Girl, word is that Boss and them left town again!" Gigi told her girl. "Is that true?"

"Who told you that, Gigi?"

"Vanity, are you serious? Boss's ass is like the emperor of this city, girl! His ass can't do shit and muthafuckas ain't watching him!"

Vanity shook her head after listening to her girl.

"Girl, yeah! His ass and Trigger left with Lloyd and Tina earlier for the airstrip," Vanity sighed.

"Where they going?" Gigi asked, unable to believe what she was hearing.

"Chicago!" Black Widow answered, causing both Gigi and Vanity to look at her.

"I'm not going to even ask how you know that since I

know Boss is crazy about you and Princess," Vanity said, rolling her eyes at Black Widow and looking back toward Gigi. "Girl, we going out to this club to get ready for tonight or what?"

~ ~ ~

After leaving Gigi's apartment and making the drive out to Club Empire, Vanity noticed that a team of Boss's men was now trailing her and Gigi in a Yukon truck. She made some calls to a few people who were supposed to perform at the club that night. She also received a number of calls from girls who she and Gigi used to dance with and that were now dancing at their club.

Once they arrived at the club, Vanity and Gigi saw that their assistants, Amy and Ebony, were already there. Vanity climbed from the front passenger seat of the Land Rover while Gigi and Black Widow stepped out of the back seats.

"Princess! Princess!" Black Widow called out to her sister after seeing her staring out at the streets.

She walked around the front end of the Land Rover and instantly spotted what had Princess's attention. She saw a Benz ML63 truck that was sitting out in front of the club.

"Who the fuck is that?" Black Widow asked while

staring at the truck.

"I don't know!" Princess answered her, still watching the Benz truck as it began slowly driving off. She then held up her hand and waved off the security Boss had assigned to Vanity.

~ ~ ~

Brandi laughed to herself as she drove off from in front of Club Empire after leaving Vanity and her so-called people watching and standing out in the parking lot. Brandi then dug out her cell phone and called Steven."

"Yeah, Brandi!"

"Hey, baby. Where are you?"

"Handling business. Why?"

"I've been checking up on the news I heard about Boss leaving town."

"Brandi!" Steven yelled. "What the fuck did I tell your ass about this punk-ass nigga, Boss? I don't give a fuck about all that shit this nigga supposedly did. His ass bleeds like I bleed, and I got something hot for his ass if he gets the fuck in my way! Now that's the last fucking time I wanna hear shit about this muthafucka! Period! Now where the fuck you at?"

Brandi was surprised at how turned on she suddenly was by the way Steven was talking to her.

"I'm on my way back to the penthouse, Steven!" she replied.

"Hurry the fuck up and get there. I want my pussy!"

Brandi slowly smiled even after hanging up with him, and she found herself actually speeding to get back to the penthouse.

~ ~ ~

Vanity was getting everything ready for the club for the night when she was interrupted by a call from the hospital letting her know Malcolm Jr. was being released. Vanity and Princess left the club and drove out to Parkway Hospital.

Once they arrived at the hospital and rode the elevator up to his floor, they stood in the doorway to his room and saw him already on his feet moving around. Moses was also in the room when they arrived.

"Malcolm!" Vanity called his name.

"What are you doing here?" Malcolm asked, after noticing Vanity.

He continued to get dressed in clothes Moses had brought for him at his request.

"Malcolm, you really shouldn't be leaving the hospital yet!" Vanity told him as she continued to watch him.

"It's been weeks!" he replied. "Besides, my baby brother is out of town, and I don't trust just anybody looking after my baby brother's lady. No disrespect, Princess!"

"You good then?" Princess questioned, showing a small smile on her face as she stared at Malcolm.

Vanity shook her head as she stood watching Malcolm finish getting changed. She walked over to help him with the black leather jacket he was putting on.

"So, where are you going, Malcolm?"

"Last time I checked, I still do have my own place!" he replied to her as he took the .45 automatic Moses walked over and handed to him.

"No!" Vanity barked while watching Malcolm slide the gun into the front of his True Religion jeans. "You're going to come to the penthouse with us until you're back to a 100 percent, okay?"

"You sure about that?" Malcolm asked her before looking over at Vanity with a questioning look.

"Just let me deal with Boss!" Vanity told him as she turned to leave the hospital room, missing Malcolm, Moses, and Princess all shaking their heads at her.

~ ~ ~

Vanity signed Malcolm out of the hospital and had Moses follow behind them. Malcolm drove with Vanity and Princess back to her penthouse. Vanity got Malcolm settled in a guest bedroom and then had Moses go by Malcolm's place to pick up some clothes for him for a few days.

"You got a really nice place here, Vanity!" Malcolm told her, catching her in of the kitchen.

Malcolm just stood at the breakfast bar and watched her.

"I'm pretty sure this isn't the only spot my baby brother has for you since he had me looking all over the city for his ass at one point!"

"You're so right! It's not!" she replied with a big smile. "Boss is very unpredictable, Malcolm!"

"I'm really starting to understand that now, Vanity!" Malcolm answered with a knowing smile.

~ ~ ~

By 6:00 p.m. Vanity was showered and dressed in a Dolce & Gabbana silk gray pantsuit as she left for the club. She smiled at the sight of the already half-filled parking lot at Club Empire. Princess pulled up in front of the club to let

Vanity out. After she stepped out, Princess then pulled off to go park the Land Rover Range Rover in her spot.

Vanity entered the club, flanked on her right and left by a team of six security guards that stood waiting for her to walk inside. Princess had called ahead and informed them of their arrival. Vanity headed through the growing crowds and walked toward the back and into her office. She shut her office door after her security team left. She barely made it over to her desk when the door that connected her office to Gigi's opened and in walked Gigi.

"I knew I heard you over here!" Gigi said, walking over to Vanity's desk dressed in a Louis Vuitton pantsuit.

She dropped a folder onto Vanity's desk.

"That's the test from the new girls you were waiting on. So what happened with Malcolm?"

"He's at the penthouse!" Vanity replied as she opened the folder.

"Whoa! What?" Gigi said in surprise. "What do you mean he's at the penthouse, Vanity? What penthouse?"

Vanity looked up from the folder she was rifling through and wasn't surprised to see the look on Gigi's face. Vanity waved her hand dismissively.

"Gigi, I do not want to hear it! Boss will have to deal with his brother staying with us until he gets better. I'm not letting that man stay at the mansion by himself!"

"You know, you're really playing with fire, Vanity!" Gigi warned her girl. "You do not know how Boss is going to react once he gets back and finds Malcolm inside his house with his woman!"

"I'll deal with Boss when he gets his ass home!" Vanity stated, just as there was a knock at her door, which caused both her and Gigi to look up.

"Yeah, Princess? What's the matter?"

"Ummm! Your man's brother is out here!" Princess announced with a small smile on her lips as she stared at Vanity's surprised face.

~ ~ ~

Malcolm Jr. entered the club dressed in a Kenneth Cole suit and surrounded by his team of soldiers, with Moses at his right. He smiled at the attention he now had focused on him compared to his last visit.

He peeped Vanity and her people as soon as she walked out onto the main floor. He held his eyes locked onto her thinking how lucky his baby brother was.

"Malcolm, what the hell are you doing here, boy?" Vanity asked as soon as she walked up to him.

She was unable to help notice that he was back to wearing his suits and looking good.

"My brother's not here, so it's my job to make sure everything is good over here!" Malcolm informed.

He went in to give Vanity a hug, only for one of her guards to place a hand on his chest.

"Relax!" Malcolm stated, just as his soldiers started to react. "Everything is good here, fellas!"

Vanity watched as Malcolm's men stepped back at his command, and then she spoke up to let her people know everything was also okay on her end. She then noticed how quiet everything became inside the club and how everyone was watching what was going on. She quickly waved to the DJ to restart the music.

"Come on, boy!" Vanity told Malcolm, motioning him and his crew as she started to lead them to the VIP section.

Once they were upstairs overlooking the stage below, Vanity had the bar send up two bottles of Ace of Spades, two bottles of Rosé, and a few more bottles for Malcolm and his crew. She then sat down and kicked it with Malcolm and

Moses for a few minutes.

"How you feeling, Malcolm?" Vanity asked as she sat next to him in front of the rail that allowed them to look down over the club's floor.

"I'm a little sore, but I'm good!" Malcolm replied as he grabbed the bottle of Ace of Spades that the half-naked server was carrying around on a tray.

He then tilted the bottle back and took a swallow.

Vanity watched Malcolm and noticed his relaxed state, but she also noticed something else that she couldn't put her finger on just yet. She then laid her hand onto his arm to get his attention.

"You take it easy with the bottles. You're supposed to be looking out for me tonight, remember?"

Malcolm smiled at Vanity and leaned over and kissed her on the cheek.

"I got you, Vanity!" he followed up.

8

Vanity was very happy with how things were going by 11:00 p.m. that night. There was a huge crowd of people inside the club, and an even larger crowd of men and women outside still trying to get in. Vanity was making her rounds throughout the club to make sure everything was going well while her guest performer, Mystikal, was making the club go wild and her girls were throwing their asses and popping pussy for that money to "Shake it Fast."

Vanity looked up to the VIP section and could see the girls she sent up to entertain Malcolm and his crew. She smiled and turned around to head back to her office, just as she heard some turmoil break out near the front door of the club. Vanity turned her attention to the door to see what was going on, only to see a large crowd pushing into the club as her security was responding to the problem.

"What the fuck is this bitch doing here?" Vanity asked out loud, after seeing Brandi with a tall, dark-brown-skinned guy.

Vanity headed directly toward the commotion when

Princess and four of her men joined her. Vanity made it through the crowd with Princess leading the way.

"What the fuck are you doing here, Brandi?" Vanity yelled once she was face-to-face with her smiling foe.

"This is a nice place you got here!" Brandi stated, looking around the club. "Too bad you're about to lose it!"

"Lose what?" Vanity asked with an attitude. "Bitch, I don't know what the fuck you think you got going on, but it's time to leave!"

"I was thinking the same thing!" Steven Wallace spoke up, drawing Vanity's attention to him. "I'm sure you got my message from her!" Steven said, nodding to Gigi, who walked up beside Vanity.

"Steven Wallace!" Vanity cried with her face balled up. "Nigga, you must have lost your damn mind! You can either get out or get carried the fuck out! You decide!"

Steven simply laughed at Vanity.

"Bitch, I wasn't asking you shit! I'm telling you to get the fuck out!"

"Naw, player!" Malcolm spoke up as he and Moses led their crew through the club and walked up beside Vanity and stopped to face Steven. "Maybe you didn't hear my sister clearly, so I'll repeat what she already told you. Leave or get put the fuck out!"

"I'd rather put them out!" Moses added as he began cracking his knuckles, with a smirk on his lips, while staring straight at Steven.

"Malcolm, you need to take your tired ass on, nigga!" Brandi interrupted before getting up in his face. "You shouldn't be saying shit when you let the next nigga take what was supposedly yours. Don't get fucked up in this shit trying to play hero to this bitch!"

"I tell you what!" everyone within earshot heard someone announce.

"Vanity, look!" Gigi whispered, tapping Vanity's arm and then pointing.

Vanity spun around in the direction Gigi was pointing, to see the crowd part. There, she saw Boss and Trigger walking through the opening and both wearing all-black Armani suits. Vanity broke out into a big smile at the sight of her man.

Boss stepped up to the right of Vanity while Malcolm stood to her left before he spoke up again.

"My wife told you something and my brother repeated

her words, but I'm just telling you, get the fuck out!"

"Nigga, who the—?" Steven began to say.

He further made the mistake of starting to step toward Boss, only to pause when what seemed like the entire club of both men and women pulled out guns and surrounded him and the crew that he had brought in with him.

Boss slowly smirked at Steven and then met his eyes once the clown had backed up from him.

"Was you about to say something, or was you getting out?"

Steven could only nod his head as he held Boss's green eyes.

"But we'll meet again!"

"You better hope we don't!" Boss said as Steven, Brandi, and their crew turned and headed toward the door.

~ ~ ~

"I tried to fucking tell your ass!" Brandi told Steven as they were driving away from the club, after just getting kicked out in front of everyone. "You thought I was just talking when I told you how Boss got the fuck down, nigga!"

Steven ignored Brandi and her mouth running off. He was in deep thought of what he wanted to do to Boss after the way he was shown up in front of everyone in the club.

"Steven!" Brandi yelled at him.

"Brandi! I'm telling you right now. Shut the fuck up!" he yelled at her with his face all balled up in anger.

"Shut the fuck up, huh?" Brandi repeated. "All right! I'ma let you get yourself killed then, since you still don't wanna listen!"

~ ~ ~

"Where the hell did you come from, nigga?" Vanity questioned Boss, once she, Boss, Malcolm, Gigi, Princess, and Black Widow were back inside Vanity's office.

"It's good to see I'm missed!" Boss joked as he walked around behind Vanity's desk and sat down in her desk chair.

"I never left from the start. I just sent Lloyd and Tina to Chicago to stay with my mom, since she's up there now!"

"Why didn't you tell me about all this?" Vanity asked with her hands on her hips while staring at Boss.

"I have my reasons!" Boss replied as he threw his feet up onto the edge of her desk.

He then looked at his brother and met Malcolm's eyes.

"I peeped how you held shit down for Vanity."

"I figure it's the most I could do since my baby brother

was out of town—or supposedly out of town!" Malcolm told Boss.

Boss nodded his head in approval and then looked over at Gigi, who asked, "Boss, where is my baby at?"

"He's handling something I asked him to handle!" Boss told her. "He'll be back, Gigi. Just relax, shorty!"

Gigi shook her head as she walked over and pushed Boss's legs from the desk. Vanity then sat down on his lap and kissed him.

"We need to talk later on!" she told him, after pulling back from his lips.

Boss nodded his head in agreement and then looked at Malcolm.

"Boss, what's the plan about this dude Steven Wallace? You do know that was probably not the last time we was gonna to see him!"

"I'm tired of that bitch Brandi too, Boss!" Vanity added, with a balled up face.

Boss slowly smiled at Vanity.

"Relax, ma! I'm already dealing with her as well speak!" Boss reassured her.

~ ~ ~

Brrrr! Brrrr! Brrrr!

Trigger let his hammer ring out as soon as the Benz limo pulled to a stop at a traffic light. He then climbed from the Nissan GT-R AMS Alpha 9 with his Glock in hand. He hit the two men who jumped out of the Escalade behind the limo, and dropped them as soon as their feet touched the ground.

Brrrr! Brrrr!

Trigger hit two more men who came running around from the passenger side of the Escalade as he continued to walk past the Escalade, even as the limo tried to pull away.

Brrrr! Brrrr! Brrrr! Brrrr!

Trigger hit the back end of the limo and blew out the back tires, which caused the limo to lose control. He then put away his Glock and pulled out his other banger as he jogged over to the limo that had smashed into a light pole. He then found Steven Wallace crawling out the back of the limo.

Brrrr!

Trigger blew away Steven Wallace in the back, leaving him slumped over half inside and half outside the limo. He then looked inside and found Brandi knocked out cold and lying across the seat.

"Let's go, bitch!" he said to himself.

Trigger grabbed Brandi by the hair and pulled her across the back seat carelessly. He tossed the heavy bitch over onto his shoulder just as Joker pulled up the Nissan in front of him. They made their get-away as police sirens could be heard drawing closer.

~ ~ ~

Boss remained with Vanity at Club Empire until closing. He then walked her out of the club once she was ready to leave, and he waited as she locked up the doors.

"Oh my God!" Vanity squealed in total disbelief after turning around and seeing the dark-indigo Rolls-Royce Wraith that was parked directly in front of the club. "Boss, what is this, boy?"

"I take it you like it?" Boss joked as he led Vanity over to the Wraith's passenger door, which he opened for her.

Vanity climbed into the Rolls-Royce onto the seashell leather seats. She smiled when she looked around the inside of the car, and then looked at Boss as he climbed behind the driver's seat.

"Boss, when did you get this?"

"I had this one and one for you ordered!" Boss told her

as he started up the Wraith. "I just had to get some work done on them before you could drive it."

"Wait! You got me one too?" Vanity exclaimed, with a huge smile on her lips.

"Of course!" Boss answered as he drove away from the club.

He then reached over to Vanity's hand and put his hand in hers as they intertwined their fingers.

"But I've got one more surprise for you right now though!"

Vanity stared at Boss a few moments and then asked, "What are you up to, Boss?"

"Oh, you'll see, ma!" he answered, winking his eye at her and causing her to smile back at him.

A little while after leaving the club, Boss pulled the Wraith in front of an old warehouse, where his team was already waiting. He parked beside the crystal-white pearl-metallic Rolls-Royce Wraith.

"Boss, what's going on?" Vanity asked as she watched Princess approach the passenger door.

"You'll see!" he replied, just as Trigger opened his door for him. He then looked over and asked, "Everything set up, baby Bruh?"

"Yup! Everything's set, big Bruh!" Trigger replied as he and Boss approached Malcolm Jr. and the others as they stood waiting for him.

Boss then took Vanity's hand and led the way into the warehouse, where two of his men were holding open the doors. They then both stepped inside.

"What the hell?" Vanity crie when she stared at the female who was stripped down to her underwear and hanging mid-air by a thick dog chain inside the middle of the warehouse. "Boss, is that who I think it is?"

Boss heard Vanity as he motioned for the woman to be lowered down to the floor. He then looked over at Vanity.

"You still feel like Brandi needs to be dealt with, ma?"

Vanity looked from a gagged Brandi over to meet Boss's green eyes, just as Princess stepped up beside her with a gun with a silencer attached to it in her outstretched hand. Vanity then looked back at Boss.

"So what do you want to do, ma? Does she live or die?"

"Kill that bitch, Vanity!" Gigi called out. "She tried to kill you and your mom, girl, remember?"

Vanity thought back to the day Gigi had brought up when

Boss got shot trying to protect her and Lloyd. She took the gun from Princess and then turned toward Brandi. She walked over to stop in front of her as the bitch began trying to say something.

"Remove the gag!"

Vanity waited and watched as one of her security removed the gag from over Brandi's mouth.

"What you gotta say, bitch?" Vanity questioned.

"You think you so fucking special, huh? Fuck you and Boss's ass!" Brandi spewed out and then laughed. "I wanna see what you gonna do when Daniels gets here and he finds out you all killed his brother. And not even Boss can stand up to him!"

"I'll let you in on a little something!" Boss spoke up as he stepped up beside Vanity and stared directly into Brandi's hateful eyes. "I know all about Daniels Wallace, the oldest son of Melinda and Daniels Wallace Sr. I've known for some time now who your little friends are, and actually I've been waiting to deal with them too!"

"Well, do you know who put Malcolm's weak ass inside the hospital, Mr. Know-It-All?" Brandi asked.

She burst out laughing when she saw the slight change

in Boss's expression, which let her know she knew something he did not.

Phisss! Phisss! Phisss!

Boss felt a little bit of the blood that spurted out from Brandi's face after three holes appeared in it. He then looked over at Vanity and saw the look on her face as he took the gun from her hand and took her into his arms.

"It's all right, ma!" Boss whispered to Vanity as he held out the gun on his left for Trigger to take from him.

9

Boss dealt with the problems of Steven Wallace and Brandi by having Brandi's body taken care of by his men and having Detective Wright handle Steven Wallace's body and the investigation. Boss then called his father and explained that their problems were being taken of, and asked him for his okay to remain in Miami to get things in order. He also found out that not only was Destiny back in Chicago, but also that his father had spoken with his wife, Patricia, and he admitted to her that he wanted a divorce, since he and Tina were getting back together.

Boss was standing out on his penthouse terrace smoking and drinking a glass of Hennessey when he heard someone walk out onto the terrace behind him.

"What's up, baby brother?" Malcolm Jr. asked, once Boss looked back over his shoulder when he heard the door slide open.

"What up?" Boss replied as Malcolm walked up beside him.

"You wanted to talk to me?" he asked as he leaned on

the rail beside his Boss and looked out over the view.

Boss handed the blunt over to Malcolm and then took a sip of his drink.

"I've been thinking. I know shit started off wrong between you and me. I know and understand that we can't make up for lost time; and truthfully, I'm not used to having a brother. But if you're willing to give this whole brother shit a chance, then I'm with it too. What you say?"

Malcolm handed the blunt back to Boss and then grabbed the glass from his hand and took a drink.

"I've always wanted a little brother! I think I can deal with the aggravation!"

Boss laughed as he pushed Malcolm playfully with his forearm.

"You dealing with aggravation, huh?"

"You is the youngest brother last I checked!" Malcolm said jokingly.

"I was also thinking!" Boss started off seriously. "How do you feel about the two of us opening up a business together?"

"What type of business?" Malcolm looked over at Boss with an odd look.

"Let's go take a ride!" Boss told his brother, pushing away from the terrace rail. "Come on!"

The brothers left the roof terrace and walked back inside the penthouse. Boss told Vanity that he and Malcolm were leaving for a little while.

"Where you about to go?" Vanity wanted to know.

Boss smiled as he kissed Vanity and said, "I'll see you in a few minutes, ma!"

Vanity watched as Boss and Malcolm walked out the front door. She walked over to the intercom in the den and called out to Trigger.

"What's up, big sis?" Trigger answered right back.

"You and Moses need to follow Boss and Malcolm. They're leaving and didn't tell me where they were heading!"

"We leaving!"

After she released the intercom button, Vanity turned around to see Gigi, Princess, and Black Widow all smiling and watching her.

~ ~ ~

Boss took the Lamborghini Huracán and flew out of the parking garage. He made the trip out to South Beach, and in a few minutes he was parking in front of a two-story building that took up three stores down the walkway.

"Hey, handsome!" both Boss and Malcolm heard once the two of them climbed from the Lambo.

They both glanced over at the group of three women, but they ignored them as the two brothers approached the building. Boss then stopped in front of the two-story building.

"This is the building I was thinking we could use for the nightclub we could open together. What do you think?"

"What do we know about running a club, baby brother?" Malcolm asked as he looked up at the building.

"I know somebody that knows about it; and if you're with the idea, we can get things started," Boss explained as he looked over at Malcolm.

Malcolm turned to face his brother and saw the serious expression on his face. Malcolm laughed lightly to himself.

"So this guy you was talking about. We splitting this shit three ways, right?"

"Pretty much!" Boss replied. "But it's a woman who I know from back in Atlanta."

Malcolm nodded his head and agreed.

"Fuck it! Let's do it, baby brother!"

Malcolm watched Boss raise his hand and wave. Malcolm then noticed the gray metallic and black BMW M5 across the street that both Trigger and Moses were now climbing out of. He then looked back at Boss.

"How the fuck did you know they were over there?"

"Trigger's always close by!" Boss admitted. "But I'm also pretty sure Vanity told him that we left the penthouse, and she made him follow us."

~ ~ ~

Boss had Trigger call their friend back in Atlanta, who was a few years older and once owned a club in the city before an accidental fire burned it down. Boss then called the number on the building for leasing or purchasing. He spoke with a John Peters about seeing the building and discussing leasing or buying it.

Afterward, Boss, Malcolm, Trigger, and Moses ate lunch at a little shop up the street from the potential new nightclub location. John Peters called back twenty minutes later to let Boss know that he was only about five minutes away, so Boss and his crew finished lunch and started walking back toward the building.

A few minutes later, a royal-blue Lincoln Continental pulled up and parked right across the street from the building. Boss stood watching with Malcolm, Trigger, and Moses as a lean, white man wearing a Polo shirt and slacks climbed from the car with a brown leather briefcase in tow.

"Mr. Holmes?" John Peters asked as he walked up to Malcolm with his hand held out for a shake.

"Actually, I'm the brother," Malcolm admitted with a smile. "The name's Warren, and this is my brother, ReSean Holmes."

"My apologies!" Mr. Peters said as he offered a smile and then put out his hand.

"Not a problem, Mr. Peters!" Boss replied, smiling back at the leasing agent.

"In fact, me and my brother are interested in looking at leasing the building. May we have a look around?"

"Of course!" Mr. Peters answered as he pulled out a set of keys from his pocket and started toward the front double doors to the building.

~ ~ ~

"Vanity!" Gigi yelled as she, Princess, Black Widow, and Erica—who had arrived at the penthouse ten minutes earlier—watched Vanity frantically pace back and forth. "Will you please sit your ass down, girl! Boss is perfectly fine. He's with not only Malcolm, but also Trigger and Moses; and you know just as well as the rest of us that all four of them men have no problem acting a damn fool if a problem appears!"

"That's not it!" Vanity told her girls, looking from Gigi to each of the other ladies in her den. "I just hate the whole fact that both Boss and Malcolm are acting like Steven Wallace's brother isn't supposed to be showing up in Miami at some point. We don't even know when this Daniels Wallace is supposedly showing up!"

"Vanity, if there's one thing I've learned about Boss," Black Widow spoke up, "it's that when it seems like he's not on point or focused on what's going on around him, that man is fully aware of everything that's going on!"

"I agree!" Princess added in agreement with her sister, just as someone's phone began to ring.

Vanity rushed over to the glass coffee table and snatched up her iPhone.

"Hello!" Vanity answered on the start of the second ring.

She listened for a few moments before saying anything.

"We coming now!" she said before she hung up the phone and then looked over at the others. "Y'all not going to believe this shit! That boy's out on South Beach, and he wants me to come out there to see the new building that both he and Malcolm are leasing to open up a new club!"

"New club?" Gigi asked.

"A nightclub, girl!" Vanity said, shaking her head and smiling.

"That man is one investing guy!" Erica stated with a smile appearing on her face as well. "Boss has more businesses opening up than I can remember, and he's not even twenty-five yet!"

"Well, let's go and see what his new investment is now!" Vanity said as she picked up her keys and Gucci purse.

~ ~ ~

Princess drove the Land Rover Range Rover and made the trip out to Miami Beach. She found the building that Boss had told Vanity about, and she noticed his Lamborghini and Trigger's BMW M5 parked across the street. Once Princess parked, Vanity was the first one out of the SUV, with Black Widow climbing out of the front passenger seat next.

"This man is talking about leasing this?" Gigi

questioned, once she was out of the Land Rover and staring up at the two-story building.

"That's what he say!" Vanity told her girl as she led the ladies across the street with Princess at her side.

Vanity entered the building first as Princess held open the door for her. The first thing she noticed was a black-painted wall as soon as she stepped inside. She followed the short hallway that led out into the building's main floor, only to see how spacious it was inside.

"Damn, Vanity!" Gigi said in shock and surprise when she saw the inside.

"Wow!" Erica added with a smile as she looked around at the impressive interior of the building.

"I take it you all are impressed?" Boss asked as he, Malcolm, and the others walked into the main floor area from the back of the building.

Boss introduced Mr. Peters to Vanity and then the other ladies. He then pulled John off to the side and had a few more words with him. Boss was handed the keys to the building and then shook hands with the businessman.

Boss then turned back toward the others as Mr. Peters headed for the exit. He tossed one of the keys to Malcolm.

"Remember, we're supposed to head out to meet back up with Peters once Steffaine gets here, big brother."

"Who's Steffaine?" Vanity wanted to know, looking back and forth between Boss and Malcolm.

"A friend from Atlanta!" Boss informed her, noticing the questioning look that appeared on her face. "Y'all wanna see the building, or what?"

"Hell yeah!" Gigi spoke up as she wrapped her arms around Trigger and then smiled brightly.

Boss took the lead and showed Vanity, Gigi, and the others through the club, which was a lot larger than they all had thought at first. It even had a kitchen in the back. Boss began telling the ladies about a few of the plans he and Malcolm had already come up with to set up inside the club, including having Collins Smokehouse cater all the food. Once the tour was over and the group was back outside where they started, Vanity was the first to speak up.

"What do you and Malcolm know about running a nightclub, Boss?"

"That's where Steffaine comes in!" Boss told her with a smile. "She knows about running a club because she ran and owned one back in Atlanta. But now we're going to offer her a second chance to run another one and become a partner in owning this club with Malcolm and me."

"Well, what are you going to name this place?" Black Widow asked Boss.

"How about Family Affair?" Erica chimed in, quickly drawing everyone's attention over to her.

Boss slowly nodded his head in approval, smiling a bit as he looked over at Malcolm.

"I like that! What you think, big brother?"

"Hmmm, Family Affair!" Malcolm repeated with a smile. "Yeah! I like it too. That's what it is then!"

10

Steffaine got everything in order in Atlanta, which allowed her to make the trip down to Miami, after accepting her friend's offer to help run a new nightclub in which she was also becoming an owner. Steffaine Rowlings followed the directions Boss had given to her, and pulled up her Lexus truck in front of the security gates of a Miami Beach high-rise apartment building.

Steffaine gave the armed guard her name as she was told to do once she arrived at the building. She was then allowed inside and easily found an open parking space. She felt a little out of place when she saw the type of cars that were parked in the lot.

Steffaine grabbed the bags she brought with her and locked up the truck. She then walked across the parking lot to the front entrance.

"Good afternoon, ma'am!" the doorman said as he opened up and held the door for Steffaine.

Steffaine spoke to the doorman as she entered the apartment building. She then looked around in amazement at how nice the lobby looked.

"May I help you, ma'am?" the woman behind the front desk asked, seeing Steffaine and the lost look she had on her face.

"Umm, I'm Steffaine Rowlings," she introduced herself to the red-headed white woman, and then explained that she was supposed to have an apartment there.

"Please hold a second, ma'am!" the woman told Steffaine while hitting the keyboard and looking at the computer screen. "Oh my, yes! Ms. Rowlings, you're here inside our platinum suite. I'll have someone come to take your bags upstairs. You also have a package and a message, Ms. Rowlings."

After waiting a few moments, Steffaine was handed a package, and a message that was written on a folded piece of paper. She then quickly read the short message which contained a phone number informing her to call Boss when she got settled.

"Ma'am!"

Steffaine looked to her right to see a bellman. She handed him her bags and then turned back to the smiling woman behind the desk, who handed the bellman a key with instructions of where to take Ms. Rowlings.

The bellman led Steffaine to the elevator, and they rode up to the seventeenth floor. Once they stepped off, he then escorted her to an oak wood front door.

"Your penthouse, ma'am," the bellman told Steffaine after unlocking the front door and then waving for her to enter first.

"Penthouse?" Steffaine repeated in a whisper as she entered the front door and stepped onto hardware floors.

She looked around in disbelief with her mouth hanging open as she stood staring at the two-story room.

"Ma'am!"

Steffaine turned back to face the bellman to see him holding out the keys to the penthouse for her. She took the keys and then thanked him.

"Will there be anything else, ma'am?" he asked her.

"No, thank you," Steffaine told the young man.

She then attempted to give him a tip, only for him to stop her and say that everything had already been taken care of for her.

After he left, Steffaine locked the door behind him and then picked up her bags from beside the door where the bellman had left them. She took her time looking through the fully furnished penthouse, starting with the chef's kitchen. She then walked through the great room with a fireplace, and then stepped into the media room with a 92-inch television.

She then went upstairs where she found two master bedrooms. She chose the room with the lanai that offered a perfect view of the water and Miami strip.

"This is amazing!" Steffaine said as she walked over to the king-sized bed and set down her bags.

She then remembered the package and began to open it. Inside she found a cell phone and a key as well as another note reminding her to call Boss.

She turned on the phone in her hand and smiled when she saw a picture of Boss and Trigger as the background photo. She then called the phone number.

"How do you like the penthouse?"

Steffaine smiled when she recognized Boss's smooth and still sexy voice.

"Boy, what exactly are you into out here that you got me up in this penthouse, Boss? You holding it like that now, huh?"

"Something like that!" Boss replied. "Go ahead and get

yourself together, and we'll be by to pick you up in an hour."

"Where we going?"

"Just dress comfortably, Steff!"

After hearing Boss hang up, Steffaine shook her head and smiled, after realizing that his ass was still the same. She tossed her new phone onto the bed and then looked at the key. She noticed the Mercedes symbol on the key, which caused her to burst out in laughter. Different ideas immediately popped into her head about just what Boss and his best friend and brother, Trigger, were into.

~ ~ ~

Steffaine dressed in dark blue Chanel jeans, a Dolce & Gabbana top that hung loose but hugged her C-cup breasts, and a pair of Dolce & Gabbana stilettos. She was brushing her shoulder-length, slightly curly black hair when her cell phone rang from inside the bedroom. She left the bathroom and grabbed the phone from the nightstand.

"Hello!"

"We outside! Come down!"

"Who is we, Boss?"

"Just come on, Steff!"

Once again after hearing Boss hang up, Steffaine sucked

her teeth as she picked up her Dolce & Gabbana bag and then left the bedroom.

After she got to the first floor of the penthouse, she turned off the lights, other than in the kitchen, since she wasn't sure when she'd be back. She then locked up and rode the elevator down to the lobby.

"Thank you!" she told the doorman as he held open the door for her as she walked out of the building, only to pause when she saw a Rolls-Royce Wraith in front.

She stood staring in disbelief as Boss climbed out from the back of the car, dressed in a cream-colored linen outfit and suede loafers.

"Damn!"

Steffaine rushed over to Boss and threw her arms around his neck. As she hugged him, she could feel his strong arms wrap around her waist. She leaned back after a moment and smiled as she looked into his green eyes that she really missed.

"Boy, look at you! You look good! You look so different with your little goatee and the wavy hair!"

"You looking good yourself, Steff!" Boss returned the compliment, after releasing her to look her over and noticing that she was thicker than she was before he left Atlanta. "Come on and let's get going!"

Steffaine climbed into the Rolls-Royce as Boss held open the back door. She looked around and could only smile.

"Boss, this is hot, boy! How can you afford something like this?"

"Things change, Steff!" Boss told her. "Let's go, baby Bruh!"

Steffaine froze when she realized who was driving behind the wheel.

"Trigger! Boy, that's you up there?"

Trigger looked back in the rear-view mirror and showed a small smile once he met up with her eyes.

"What's up, Steffaine?"

"Boy, look at you up there!" Steffaine cried out as she sat forward and hugged Trigger from the back, wrapping her arms around his neck and kissing him on the cheek.

Boss smiled, watching Steffaine until she released Trigger.

"Steff, listen! We about to meet up with my brother, Malcolm, real—!"

"Whoa!" Steffaine said, cutting off Boss and holding her

hand up. "What do you mean, your brother, Boss? You had Trigger tell me that same thing, and the only brother I've known you to have is Trigger. Who's this brother you're telling me about?"

"You gonna let me finish?" Boss asked with a smile.

"Talk, nigga!" Steffaine goaded him, waving Boss on to continue.

Boss laughed and shook his head, since he realized that Steffaine hadn't changed at all. He looked up to the front of the car, only to see Trigger was even smiling and shaking his head as well.

~ ~ ~

By the time Boss's Rolls-Royce was finally pulling into Collins Smokehouse, Malcolm Jr. was just stepping out of the restaurant behind Moses, only to pause and have a change of heart at the sight of the Wraith.

"I guess we staying after all, huh?" Moses asked with a smirk as he looked over at his boss and friend.

Malcolm ignored Moses's comment as he looked at his rose-gold presidential Rolex watch and saw that Boss was an hour late, when he said it would only be thirty minutes.

"Damn!"

Malcolm looked over at Moses after hearing him but noticed him staring at something. Malcolm followed his best friend's gaze only to lock in and stare at the woman who was climbing out of the back of Boss's Wraith.

"God damn!"

Malcolm was still staring at the woman when Trigger and Boss escorted her over to where he and Moses stood waiting. Malcolm never heard anything Boss said, as he was too busy staring at the female.

Boss chuckled lightly when he saw the way Malcolm was looking at Steffaine.

"Big brother, you good?" Boss asked, waving his hand in front of Malcolm's face.

"Y-yeah!" Malcolm could barely get out as he looked over at Boss and then shifted his eyes back to Steffaine.

"Steffaine, this is my older brother who I told you about!" Boss introduced as he stood up and smiled.

Steffaine was very surprised at how much alike Boss and his brother looked, other than the green eyes and full beard. She also couldn't help but notice the way Malcolm was staring at her.

"It's good meeting you, Malcolm."

"I was just thinking the same exact thing, Steffaine," Malcolm blurted out, smiling flirtatiously while holding her eyes and getting a smile out of her.

~ ~ ~

Once they were inside the restaurant and seated away from the crowd, which was difficult since the place was always busy, Boss, Malcolm Jr., Steffaine, Trigger, and Moses sat down and had a casual conversation. They all got to know each other better while they waited for their food to arrive.

Steffaine sat listening to Boss and Malcolm's story about how the two first met up, until the point when they found out that they were actual brothers by blood.

"So now you two want to become business partners, huh?" Steffaine inquired as she kept a close eye on Malcolm Jr., since she had an interest in him for some reason. "What's the name of this supposed new club you two are thinking of opening?"

"Family Affair!" Boss replied proudly.

Steffaine slowly nodded her head and repeated the name to herself.

"Okay, I like it. But how does the building look, and is it

in a good area?"

The food arrived, so Boss waited until Gina set the plate down, accepting a kiss on his cheek before she walked away. He then continued.

"Just who was that?" Steffaine asked in surprise at the open show of affection Boss allowed.

"A close friend!" Boss answered as he picked up his fork. "As for the question you asked. The building is two stories and extra wide, and it sits in the middle of Miami Beach facing the water on a busy street surrounded by other businesses."

"But what makes you think this spot is a good one for a nightclub," Steffaine asked, looking from Boss over to Malcolm and then back to Boss.

"That's where you come into play, Steff," Boss began, in all seriousness. "I've seen what you can do, and I know you can make this happen. Look at it this way, Steff. This club is as much yours as it is ours, since we're going to be partners and everything splits three ways. So what do you say?"

Steffaine could only shake her head as she stared at Boss and then looked over at Malcolm, only to see the smirk on his handsome face.

"I'm agreeing to this, but I don't want or need you two in my way. Period! Are we clear on that?"

"Perfectly!" both Malcolm and Boss said in unison while smiling at Steffaine.

11

Boss kept his word to Steffaine and stayed out of her way after the three of them signed all the necessary paperwork Mr. Peters required for ownership of the building. Boss then turned his attention to his other businesses, first by checking up with Eazy and the rest of the crew to make sure business was still being run and there were no problems. He next made a call to April to re-up on roxies, and then he reached out to his boy Murphy to re-up on the coke. But like the roxies, he requested a much larger order of coke than the last time, since he was also shipping Blue Devils back to his father in Chicago to keep business flowing that way as well.

Boss called his father after hanging up with Murphy. He then walked out to the roof terrace of his penthouse and listened as the line rang once and then twice.

"Hello!"

Boss paused for a split second and then smiled when he recognized the voice who answered the phone.

"Pops letting you answer his phone now, Mom?"

"I don't need permission! But how you doing, Mr.

Holmes, since you don't know how to call and see how your mother is doing?"

"Mom, I'm sorry! I've just been busy dealing with a few issues down here in Miami. How are you doing up there anyway, beautiful?"

"It's really nice here, baby, and I'm really beginning to like it a lot more than Atlanta. When are you coming back up here?"

"I should be out that way soon. I'm kind of in the middle of getting a new business up and running, Mom."

"Another one?"

"Yeah!"

"What's it this time, ReSean?"

"A nightclub."

"Boy, you are—!"

Boss heard his father in the background interrupting his mother. He smiled when his mother announced that she was passing the phone to Malcolm Sr.

"What's up, Son?"

"What up, Pops?"

"How's everything going down there?"

"So far, so good for the moment," Boss admitted before

he further explained about his concerns in dealing with Daniels Wallace supposedly showing up in the city and finding out what had happened to his brother.

"So that little problem has been taken care of then?" Malcolm asked.

"What problem, Pops?" Boss said with a smirk.

"I see!" Malcolm replied with a smirk on his lips as well.

"How's everything with business out that way?" Boss asked his father. "Everything with Jones and Edwins okay?"

"For the moment, it's quiet," Malcolm Sr. replied. "Speaking of those two, do you remember our last conversation?"

"I remember," Boss answered. "You and Rachell take care of that?"

"They're being viewed as we speak."

Boss remained quiet for a moment and then spoke up again in code. He told his father that he was sending him another shipment of Blue Devils. He added that he was also sending two of his people there to make sure everything was in order and to do what was needed.

"I'll send the jet down there, Son!"

Boss spoke with his father a little longer before asking

about Lloyd and Tina. They then got on the subject of his mother. But before hanging up, Boss mentioned what he and Malcolm Jr. had going on, to which he received his father's approval.

Boss smiled after hanging up with his father, and then decided to hit up his brother to see what he was doing.

~ ~ ~

Malcolm Jr. climbed out of the back of his Benz truck that was parked in front of the soon-to-be nightclub building of which he was part owner. He spotted Steffaine's new drop-top Mercedes-Benz E350 that Boss had bought for her. He and Moses then crossed the street just as his cell phone began to ring.

Malcolm saw that Boss was calling, so he answered the phone.

"What's up, baby brother?"

"What's up? Where you at?"

"Umm. Checking on something. Why? Everything cool with you, little brother?"

"Yeah!" Boss answered. "After you finish, come by the penthouse."

"I got you!"

"And tell Steffaine I said what's up!"

Malcolm could only laugh after hearing Boss's comment right before he hung up. He was still unable to understand just how the hell the boy seemed to always know what was going on with everyone. Malcolm slid the phone back into his pocket and then nodded to Moses, who stepped ahead and opened up the door to the club. Malcolm walked inside to hear construction work going on.

He looked around and saw men working throughout the building. He felt Moses tap him on the shoulder and then nod over to where Steffaine was standing. She was talking with a black man who was doing too much smiling for Malcolm's taste. Malcolm started to head toward Steffaine and walked up behind her, catching the worker's eyes, who quickly stopped smiling when he saw the stare Malcolm was giving him.

"Mr.—Mr. Warren, sir!" the worker stumbled, after recognizing Malcolm and Moses standing behind Steffaine.

Steffaine could see and hear the fear in the head construction worker, Jason's, face and voice. She spun around to see Malcolm standing behind her. She then gave Jason a hard look that had the man shaken up.

"Malcolm, what are you doing here?"

"I actually came to see if you wanted to go get lunch!" Malcolm requested before he turned to the construction worker. "Don't you got work to do, or are you ready to leave not necessarily the same way you walked up in this shit? You get me?"

"Y-yes sir, Mr. Warren, sir!" Jason answered before rushing to get back to work.

Steffaine watched Jason's reaction to Malcolm, and she quickly lost interest after seeing how weak he allowed himself to become in Malcolm's presence. She then turned back to Malcolm with an attitude.

"Look here, Malcolm! I don't know who you think you are or why this soft-ass dude is acting like he's all shook up by the sight of you, but like I told you and Boss before, stay out of my way!"

"And I heard you!" Malcolm responded with a smirk. "But like I just said, I wanted to take you out to lunch. So are you coming or not?"

Steffaine stared at Malcolm with her hands up on her hips and faced balled up.

She planned on telling him to get the fuck out, but instead

she heard herself say, "Let me get my shit, Malcolm!"

Malcolm smiled as he watched Steffaine walk off. He certainly approved of the sexy sway of her hips and her 34-26-38 curvy frame.

~ ~ ~

"Where are we going, Malcolm?" Steffaine asked once she was seated next to him in the back of his G-Wagen truck while Moses pulled away from in front of the club.

"Do you like seafood?" he asked, looking over at her. "We're going to this place called Crab House."

Steffaine rolled her eyes at Malcolm while he sat next to her with a big smile. She actually wasn't really mad; but she didn't want him thinking he could have his way, even though she realized she was inside his truck allowing him to take her out for lunch.

"Tell me something, Steffaine," Malcolm began his questioning, trying to get her attention after seeing that she refused to look at him, yet knowing that she had heard him. "What's it gonna take?"

"Excuse me?" she asked with a balled-up face as she swung her head around to look at Malcolm.

Malcolm simply ignored the attitude she was giving him.

"I'm not one to play around with words. I get straight to the point when it's something I want to say or when it's something I want—and in this case, it's you I want!"

"Me, huh?" Steffaine asked before she laughed in his face. "And what makes you think I'm even interested in you, or that you even have a chance with me?"

"Do I?" Malcolm boldly asked.

"My focus isn't on starting anything with anyone new right now, Malcolm. I'm trying to open our new club, if you remember!"

Malcolm could only nod his head.

"I can respect that!"

Steffaine expected Malcolm to continue and not give up that easily. She was about to say something else, but then decided against it and just kept quiet.

~ ~ ~

Once they arrived at Crab House and the two of them were seated, Moses took a seat at a table a few feet away. Malcolm and Steffaine then sat quietly for a few moments after the server left.

"What do they have good here?" Steffaine asked, breaking the silence between the two of them.

She then began looking at her menu while Malcolm did the same.

"Depends on your taste!" he answered. "The snow crabs are good!"

"What are you having?"

"The steak and shrimp platter," Malcolm replied, just as the owner appeared.

Steffaine looked up at the middle-aged white man who seemed extremely happy to see Malcolm. The owner asked about Boss and wanted to know if he would be stopping by as well. Steffaine had no doubt in her mind that both Malcolm and Boss were really a lot more major than the two of them tried to let on.

Once the owner left their table, Malcolm looked back at his menu only to hear Steffaine ask, "So, that's what I have to deal with if I was to ever decide I wanted anything with you?"

"What's that?" Malcolm replied, only to hear Steffaine suck her teeth before rolling her eyes at him.

She then focused back on her menu as Malcolm slowly smiled while watching her.

12

Two weeks after their first lunch at Crab House, which turned into a regular date between the two of them no matter what they were doing or where they were, Steffaine actually found herself looking forward to those lunches with Malcolm Jr.

Steffaine was also looking forward to completing club Family Affair. She was very happy at how quickly things were moving along with the building construction as well as her dealings with the liquor supplier and the DJ to whom Vanity had introduced her. Steffaine checked her Casio watch and saw that it was ten minutes before she was supposed to meet up with Malcolm for lunch. She got herself ready and was outside the club a few minutes later. She was walking to her car when a pearl-white, late-model 1956 Bentley S-1 Continental slowly pulled up beside her.

Steffaine watched the black window on the old-school Bentley slide down, which allowed the middle-aged white man in the back seat to be seen. She stopped in front of her car and turned to face the man.

"Can I help you?"

"Actually, young lady, you can!" the man with an Italian accent replied, just as the Bentley came to a complete stop. "I have been meaning to come by and speak with you, miss!"

"And who exactly are you, and why do you need to speak with me?" Steffaine asked, with an attitude beginning to show.

The man slowly smiled at her.

"My name, young lady, is Galile. Antonio Galile! And we need to speak concerning a deal that needs to be discussed with the business you are planning to open on my strip!"

Steffaine stared at the old man as if he was completely out of his mind. She began to laugh, unable to believe what the hell she was hearing from him.

~ ~ ~

Malcolm checked his Rolex for the fifth time while waiting for Steffaine to arrive at the restaurant. She was ten minutes late. Malcolm sighed deeply as he shook his head. He looked over at Moses a few tables away and nodded to let him know that he was ready to go. As Malcolm stood up from his seat, Moses walked over and dropped a few bills onto the table before following him toward the car.

Malcolm pulled out his cell phone as he was stepping out of the soul food restaurant that Steffaine had suggested they try. He pulled up her number and was listening to it ring, when he looked up and saw her Benz turning into the parking lot.

He hung up his phone and then slid it back into his pocket as he made his way over toward her Mercedes. He instantly spotted the expression on her face and quickened his steps over toward her.

"Steffaine, what happened?" Malcolm questioned as he grabbed her before realizing what he was doing. "Did something happen at the club? Did somebody do something to you? What's up, baby?"

"Malcolm, we have a problem!" Steffaine began to explain, staring into his eyes.

"What's the problem," he asked, balling up his face, yet all ready to get rid of whatever it was immediately.

Steffaine told Malcolm about the surprise visit she received from the Italian man who introduced himself as Antonio Galile. She further explained to him about his demands that they split the profits with his family for the use of having a business on what he claimed was their strip. If they didn't comply, Galile would shut down the nightclub within a few days.

"Shut down the club, huh?" Malcolm repeated with a little chuckle. "You got this guy's info?"

Steffaine shook her head no.

"He said he would be by tomorrow at noon for the first week's payment."

Malcolm simply nodded his head.

"Don't worry about it! I'ma take care of it!"

~ ~ ~

Malcolm rescheduled his lunch date with Steffaine and sent her back to the club, with Moses to watch over her. He then called ahead and found out that Boss was with Eazy at their stash spot in Murder Grove. Malcolm drove his S63 coupe out to the spot and saw his brother's Porsche parked out in front of the apartment, along with Eazy's Benz and Savage's Ford F350 Excursion nearby.

After parking, Malcolm entered the building. He approached the apartment, where a team of two shooters was posted. He received nods from both men as they stepped aside allowing him inside.

"What's good, fam?" Eazy called out as he was walking out of the kitchen just as Malcolm was walking through the front door.

Malcolm nodded in response to Eazy as he walked right past him into the front room to find Boss with Trigger and Savage counting money on the machine. He got straight to the point and never even sat down.

"Baby brother, we got a problem!"

Boss looked up from the stack of cash that was next to go into the bill counter and met his brother's eyes. He could see by his expression that it was something important.

"What up, Malcolm? Who's the problem?" Trigger jumped in.

"The Galile family," Malcolm answered, looking back at his brother. "I called and had this guy, Antonio Galile, checked out, and found out that he's the son of George Galile."

"I've heard that name before," Eazy said, drawing attention to himself. "He's supposed to be some type of low-level mob boss who moved from California and supposedly set up shop in South Beach."

"So now he's trying to step down on our business!"

Malcolm stated. "I'm not wasting time with this shit! Steffaine said he's supposed to show up tomorrow for the first week's payment, but I'ma have something for his ass instead."

"Relax, big brother!" Boss finally spoke up after thinking and listening to what the hell was being told to him. "Let's not jump straight into a war without knowing what we're up against. Do you at least have a contact number for this guy, Antonio Galile?"

"Steffaine said he didn't leave one, just that he would be by to pick up payment tomorrow at noontime," Malcolm informed his brother, just as someone's phone began to ring.

Malcolm looked at his brother, to see him pull out his phone and then crack a smile.

"Pops, what's up?" Boss said as he stood from his seat, motioning Malcolm Jr. to follow him as they both walked out of the front room and into one of the two back rooms in the apartment.

~ ~ ~

Boss and Malcolm spoke to their father about the Galile family, to which he instantly recognized the name and warned them about backing off from going to war with the family. The brothers heard their father's suggestion; however, they both ignored the warning. They refused to close down the club before it opened or pay for permission to run their club on the strip that the Galile family supposedly owned.

After the phone call with their father, both Boss and Malcolm came up with an easy decision on which they both agreed. Boss began hatching a plan for tomorrow at noon for their supposed first-payment meeting with Antonio Galile.

13

Steffaine was nervous as the time continued to pass and 12:00 noon got closer. She tried to focus on the paperwork she was looking over inside her office above the club. But as she tried to read the documents, she gave up after a few moments, tossed the papers aside, and sighed out loud.

She stood up from her desk and walked over to the tinted window that overlooked the main floor of the club below, just as the light from the front entrance doors shined through. A few moments later Malcolm appeared in her view, dressed handsomely in a metallic gray silk suit with what looked like twenty or thirty men with him. Steffaine couldn't help the smile that appeared on her lips at the simple sight of him. She left her office and took the elevator down to the floor and walked out to meet him.

"What's up, gorgeous?" Malcolm said, smiling at the sight of her in her Gucci pants suit that perfectly hugged her body.

Steffaine walked right up to Malcolm and hugged his

neck. She kissed his cheek and then asked, "What took you so long to get here, boy?"

"I missed you too!" Malcolm replied with a grin.

He and Steffaine turned around to see Boss walk in wearing an all-white suit with no tie and talking on the phone. Trigger was right behind him wearing all-black, and he looked like he was ready to get into something.

"What are you two up to, Malcolm?" Steffaine asked, looking from Boss and Trigger back to Malcolm.

Malcolm winked at her and gave her a small smile. He then looked from her back over to Boss.

"We ready, big brother?"

"Everything set up?" Malcolm stated, just as one of his men walked up beside him and whispered into his ear.

Malcolm smiled and looked over at Boss.

"It's showtime, baby brother!"

~ ~ ~

Steffaine took the lead at Boss's request and headed for the front doors, only to have two of Malcolm and Boss's men hold them open for her. She stepped outside to see all of Malcolm's men and even more men crowding the street while a dark blue Lincoln Navigator sat in the middle of the street. But instead of seeing the same middle-aged Antonio Galile, she saw a younger man dressed in a black suit, white dress shirt, and black tie. He had two tall and muscular men standing to his right and left.

"This is not the same guy from yesterday!" Steffaine whispered to Malcolm and Boss, who were standing on her left and right.

"I know!" Boss stated as he allowed her to walk ahead while he and Malcolm stayed only a few feet behind her.

"What's all of this?" the younger Italian guy asked, looking around at all the men out on the street and surrounding his SUV.

"Who are you?" Steffaine asked the young man while ignoring his question.

"Name's Antonio Galile Jr.," he replied. "I'm here to pick up this week's payment. My father explained to you how much, correct?"

"It's not happening!" Boss spoke up, drawing Antonio Jr.'s attention over to him.

"Who the hell are you?" he asked, looking over at Boss.

The young man was just about to say something else, only to be interrupted by the other man standing next to

Boss.

"Go back to your father and make sure you repeat what I'm about to tell you!" Malcolm told Antonio Jr. "We're not looking for problems, but we know how to deal with our problems. We hope it does not lead to problems, but there will be no payments now or for as long as our business is in this location!"

"There will be no negotiation," Boss spoke up again. "And tell your father that Boss said that!"

"You're all making a big mistake!" Antonio Jr. said with a smile as he climbed back into the back of the Navigator.

Boss watched as the SUV pulled off and his men opened up an area to allow it to pass through. Boss looked over at Steffaine and saw her worried expression, only to wink his eye at her and smile.

~ ~ ~

"Yeah, Papa! We've got a problem with that nigga bitch from whom I was supposed to pick up her first payment."

"What could this young woman possibly do to cause a problem, Tony?"

"That's just it, Papa! She has these two nigga boys who were with her when I arrived," he explained.

He then provided more details about what had happened when he arrived at the club to retrieve the payment.

There was complete silence after Antonio Jr. told his father about the incident that had happened moments ago. He also gave his father the message that Boss wanted him to pass along to him.

"I will send them a message and see then if they will reconsider their decision, Antonio Sr. said, to which Antonio Jr. cracked a smile.

After hanging up with his father, Antonio Jr. was still smiling. He stared out the window and thought about the pretty little black bitch that was at the meeting. However, he was so caught up in his thoughts that he never noticed the dark shadow-gray Porsche 911 Carrera that was tailing him a few cars back.

~ ~ ~

Boss walked into his office, which was located in between Steffaine's and Malcolm's offices. He sat back in his tall, black leather chair behind his wide, black wood desk, and listened somewhat to the discussion Steffaine and Malcolm were having concerning the Galile family.

"Steffaine!" Boss interrupted her and Malcolm as he got

their attention. "I know you're not going to like it, but from now on, you're going to have men trailing you for protection everywhere you go."

"Boss, I am not!"

"Relax, shorty!" Boss told her, holding up his hand for her to hold on. "They are there only for your protection, which means they will not interfere at all with how you go about your day, unless you need them."

Steffaine sucked her teeth and started to speak again, when someone's phone began to ring. She wasn't surprised when Boss pulled out his cell phone.

"Yeah!" Boss said, after answering the call from Trigger.

"We're on him now, big Bruh! He's at some chick's crib now!"

"Hold your spot and keep a—!" Boss stopped in mid-sentence over the phone.

He jumped to his feet along with Malcolm as Steffaine hit the floor, after the familiar sounds of semi-automatic guns started to fire. Boss took off from behind his desk at the same time Malcolm knocked over his chair he was sitting in and took off as well.

Both brothers ran down the steps two at a time, and made

it to the main floor in less than a minute. They broke off into a sprint, and both had their hammers out by the time they burst through the front doors of the club. They watched as a white van flew up the street and swung around the corner. Boss looked back at the building and saw the bullet holes that were everywhere, while Malcolm looked at all the spent shells all over the street.

"Boss!"

Boss spun around at the sound of Steffaine's voice to see Malcolm rushing to her. He then looked around and saw all the people on the street staring at the scene. He shook his head and thought all that bullshit wasn't good for business.

"Boss, here!" Steffaine said as she and Malcolm walked up beside him and she handed him a cell phone. "You left it on the floor when you ran out of the office. Trigger's still on the phone."

"Baby Bruh!" Boss said into the phone, after taking the phone from Steffaine.

"Big Bruh, what's up? Everything good out there?"

"Yeah! But forget what I told you about watching that punk muthafucka! Let that bastard get some rest. You feeling me!"

"No doubt, big Bruh!"

After hanging up with Trigger, Boss looked back at Malcolm and Steffaine as they stood watching him.

"I gave my warning, but this pasta-eating muthafucka seems like he ain't listening. So fuck 'im! I'ma end this shit before it gets out of hand and fucks up business!"

~ ~ ~

Brrrr! Brrrr! Brrrr! Brrrr!

Boom! Boom! Boom!

"What the hell!" Antonio Jr. yelled as he pushed the young bitch off of him while she was on her knees in front of him sucking his dick.

Antonio Jr. first heard what sounded like a door being kicked in, but he soon recognized the sounds of guns being fired inside the house. He jumped off the bed and rushed to put on his clothes.

Brrrr!

Aaaahhhhhhh1

Antonio Jr. screamed in extreme pain after his legs were ripped from underneath him. He hit the ground hard face-first.

"Shut that bitch up!" Trigger barked at the white, red-haired girl who was screaming and balled up on the floor.

Boom! Boom! Boom!

Rico did as Trigger had asked and dumped three rounds into the young girl, silencing her ass forever. He then looked back at Trigger and saw his boy pull a cell phone from Antonio Jr.'s pants pocket and begin taking pictures with his phone.

Brrrr! Brrrr! Brrrr!

Rico watched as Trigger opened homeboy back open with the banger that he kept on him at all times, which he followed up by taking more pictures. Rico shook his head as he watched a big smile appear on Trigger's face.

"Let's get the fuck outta here!" Trigger shouted to Rico as they both turned to leave.

However, Trigger turned around once more.

Brrrr!

14

Antonio Galile Sr. shed tears after receiving the before and after murder pictures of his only son taken from his own phone, only later to receive a phone call from his son's phone from the young man who introduced himself as Boss. Galile sat and listened for a while to the young nigga's cocky way he spoke to him, until he could listen no longer, so he simply hung up on Boss.

"What are you going to do, sir?" Antonio Sr. heard his bodyguard and right-hand man ask him.

Galile sat quietly for a moment and thought of his next order of action, just as his phone began to ring once more.

He waved for his bodyguard to answer the call while he continued thinking, until his man held out the phone for him.

"Who is it?"

"Mr. Galile, sir!" the bodyguard said.

Taking the phone from his bodyguard, Antonio Sr. placed it to his ear.

"Yes, Father!"

"Antonio, what's going on out there in Miami?"

"What do you mean, Father?"

"I'm sure you know exactly what I am speaking of. I just received a call from Malcolm Warren Sr. expressing his concerns about a war that neither he nor I want to happen."

"Father, what are you talking about?" Antonio Sr. asked in confusion. "There is no war between us and the Warren family. But I will be dealing with one of these young nigga boys out here. He calls himself Boss."

"That's who I'm talking about, Antonio!" Mr. Galile informed his son. "This young Boss is Malcolm Warren Sr.'s youngest son; and from what I have gathered, this boy is worse than his father. But he is not alone. He is with Malcolm Warren Jr. So I'm asking you to forget whatever problem has happened and leave these young men alone, Antonio!"

"You seriously are asking me to forget and leave the young fools alone who murdered your grandson?" Antonio Sr. asked his father. "I will kill this son of a bitch for murdering my only son. And that is final, Father!"

~ ~ ~

After George Galile heard his son hang up the phone, he loudly sighed and shook his head. He could already see the major problem his son was going to face in Miami. He could do nothing but make a call back to Malcolm Warren Sr. about the news he had just received.

"Hello!"

"Warren, it's Galile!"

"Have you spoken with Antonio?"

George sighed again.

"Warren, it seems we have a really big problem on our hands. From what Antonio has told me, your son has already acted and has murdered Antonio's son—and now Antonio wants revenge."

"George, I mean no disrespect, but if you can't talk Antonio down, things may not end well for him. My son, Boss, isn't your normal young man. This boy is extremely bright and is an extremely great thinker, and he has no problem doing things most people wouldn't want to do—

myself added. I will try to speak with both of my sons, but I will not tell them to allow Antonio to do them harm. So I beg you to talk with Antonio again. Please!"

~ ~ ~

After hanging up with George Galile and calling Boss's phone, Malcolm Sr. received his voice mail. He then hung up and called Malcolm Jr.'s phone.

"Yeah, Malcolm!" his oldest son answered at the start of the second ring.

"Malcolm, where is your brother?"

"He's right here! What's up?"

"Put ReSean on the phone."

"Malcolm, we're kind of in the middle—!""Boy, put Boss on the fucking phone!" Malcolm, Sr. screamed, cutting his son off.

Malcolm heard his youngest son's voice after the phone was exchanged.

"Yeah, Pop! What's up?"

"Boss, I thought you weren't going to start a war, Son!

What in the hell happened?"

Malcolm Sr. listened to his youngest son get straight to the point and explained that Antonio had made the first move by sending a gun team to shoot up the club while he, Malcolm Jr., and Steffaine—his business partner—were all inside the building. Malcolm Sr. then spoke up once Boss was done.

"Boss, listen! I spoke with Antonio's father, George; and from what he is saying, Antonio wants revenge for his son's murder."

"Well, it's too bad. Because he's soon to be next on my list, since both he and his son were real careless with information, Pops! I'll tell you this and we're done with this conversation: Antonio Galile has less time to live then he knows. Watch *World News* tonight, Pops. I gotta go!"

Malcolm Sr. heard his son's threat and fully understood what the boy was saying. He knew Boss had already sent a hit team to take out Antonio Galile. Malcolm set down his phone and picked up the television remote, just as Brenda walked into the bedroom with her new cell phone.

~ ~ ~

Malcolm Sr. was unsure exactly when he had fallen asleep, but he woke from the sound of his cell phone ringing beside his head. He opened his eyes to darkness and saw his cell phone light up on the bedside table.

"Malcolm, you're phone is ringing, baby," Brenda told him half asleep.

He picked it up and saw that Boss was calling him again, so he answered.

"Yeah, Son!"

"You watching the news?"

"No! Why?"

"Turn on *World News*, Pops!"

Upon hearing Boss's demand, Malcolm Sr. picked up the remote and turned on the wall-unit television.

"Malcolm, what are you doing, baby?" Brenda asked her husband, looking up at the television that he had just turned on.

Malcolm Sr. heard Brenda, but remained silent after seeing Antonio Galile's picture on the television screen. He sat listening to the news report about Antonio's murder by the explosion of some type of man-made device that the police were still investigating.

"Jesus Christ!"

"I take it you're watching the news report, Pops!" Malcolm Jr. heard Boss ask their father while Malcolm Jr. was still watching it himself.

Malcolm Sr. just shook his head in amazement.

"Boss! Boy, you are something else, Son! I'm not going to even ask how you were able to set this up, but just try to stay out of any more trouble, Son! I'll deal with George Galile!"

"Thanks, Pops, and tell Mom and said I love her!" Boss told his father before hanging up the phone.

15

Steffaine was extremely surprised at how great things were turning out at the grand opening of the club. She squeezed her way through the crowd at club Family Affair, speaking with numerous guests and greeting VIPs. Celebrities joining the crowd of guests included athletes as well as members of the pop, R&B, and rap world. Steffaine was very surprised that Boss and Malcolm were known by so many people at that level.

Steffaine felt a hand gently grab hers with enough strength that she looked back to see that it was one of her two security guards Boss had assigned to her. She leaned in to hear what he was saying.

"Boss and Malcolm are here!"

Steffaine nodded her head and then exited the VIP section and headed toward the elevator. She went downstairs to the main level and was just stepping off when she heard the announcement of the arrival of Boss and Malcolm Warren Jr.

She heard the entire club begin to yell and scream at Boss

and Malcolm's arrival. She could do nothing but smile when she saw the two of them dressed in identical silk, white and light gray pinstripe suits. Boss wore a matching stylish hat that really brought out the outfit. She allowed both of her security guards to open a path for her through the crowd, until she reached Boss and Malcolm and their crews.

"There she goes!" Malcolm said, smiling once he saw Steffaine.

He looked her over in the tight, body-hugging Chanel dress she had on. He caught her by surprise when he grabbed her by the waist and pulled her up against him. He laid a kiss on her that caused her body to catch fire.

"Well, damn!" Princess said, causing everybody to laugh as they stood watching Malcolm and Steffaine.

Steffaine returned the kiss just as hungrily.

"You two wanna save that for some other time?" Boss asked with a smile while Vanity stood beside him smiling and holding his hand.

After catching her breath and sighing after she and Malcolm ended their lip-lock, Steffaine shook her head, trying to hide her smile as she looked away from Malcolm to meet Boss's smiling green eyes.

"Ummm, the owners' box is set up for you all, and there are a few guests in the VIP area here to see you two."

The brothers allowed Steffaine to lead the way as they took the elevator in three groups while the rest of the crew decided to either take the stairs or stay downstairs. The owners' box was surprisingly wide and set up with suede sofas and couches that faced the floor-to-ceiling glass windows that overlooked the club. Boss walked over to the sofa and saw an ashtray that had four already rolled blunts and a bottle of Ace of Spades and Hennessey sitting on the round side table.

"This is really nice, babe!" Vanity said as she sat down beside Boss, looked around, and was greatly impressed. "Steffaine really did a great job with this place."

"She did a hell of a job with this place!" Gigi yelled over to Vanity from her spot on top of Trigger's lap, smiling while she looked all around her.

"Boss!" Steffaine said, getting his attention. "I don't

know how you knew this place was going to be a gold mine, but it's only 10:00 p.m. and we're already packed out and past our estimate we thought we'd pull in for our opening night!"

Boss dug out his vibrating phone while listening to Steffaine. He glanced down at his phone and saw that Detective Wright was calling him. He held up his hand for Steffaine to hold on a minute. Boss then stood up from his spot on the sofa, walked over to the glass, and answered the call.

"What's up, Cop?"

"Boss, you've got ten minutes!" Detective Wright warned him. "What we've talked about is about to happen. They've got a witness, and now they have an arrest warrant for you!"

"This witness! Do you know who it is?" Boss asked as he stood looking over the floor down below at all the party-goers.

"I'm looking into that now. But with the ATF and the FBI fighting for this arrest, I'm having a little trouble getting any information. But I've got somebody that's in the Bureau that may be able to help me out!"

"You find this witness and find out what they have, and I've got $2 million for you!" Boss informed the detective before he hung up and turned around and called Malcolm.

"What's up, baby Brother?" he said as he walked up beside Boss with a smile and dropped his arm around his shoulder.

"Big Brother, listen! I've got less than ten minutes before both the FBI and ATF run up inside of here to arrest me. Relax!" Boss started, seeing that his brother was about to snap. "Everything is already being worked on as we speak. But I'ma need you to do two things. Make sure you stay in contact with Detective Wright. He's going to call your phone since I gave him your number as a contact. And then I'ma need you to contact Pops and let him know I may need his help."

"What about Vanity?"

"She already knows what's going on! I've already warned her!"

"Wait! How long have you known that you were under investigation?"

"A few weeks now!"

Boss and Malcolm heard the screams, which immediately drew both their attention. They stood up and looked down onto the main floor as both the FBI and ATF rushed into the club, causing a huge scene.

"What the hell!" Steffaine yelled as she, Vanity, and the others all rushed over to where Boss and Malcolm were standing. She stood in shock as the FBI and ATF laid down the people inside the club. "What the hell is going on?"

"I got it, Steff!" Boss reassured her as he looked over to Steffaine and winked his eye at her, smirking.

Boss turned his attention over to Vanity, who stood watching him. He then leaned and gave her a kiss.

"I'll see you in a little bit, beautiful!" he whispered.

~ ~ ~

Vanity watched her man and his brother leave the owners' box and take the elevator down to the main floor. She stood with her crew and watched through the glass floor-to-ceiling window as the elevator door opened and out stepped Boss followed by Malcolm. She broke out into a small smile when she heard the power and strength in her man's voice when he raised his voice in a booming tone that got the attention of the FBI and ATF agents.

She continued to watch Boss as he walked away from Malcolm after the two embraced one another. Vanity then caught Boss's eyes as he glanced back up at her and winked before allowing the federal agents to grab and handcuff him.

"Vanity, what's going on?" Erica asked as she walked away from Eazy and moved up beside Vanity.

"Nothing!" Vanity answered as she looked over to Erica with a smile. "Boss has everything under control."

~ ~ ~

The federal agents left with Boss and a few of his men, who acted up when they saw him being placed in handcuffs. Afterward, Malcolm, Trigger, Eazy, Princess, Black Widow, Vanity, Steffaine, Moses, Joker, Savage, and Rico all sat inside Malcolm's office as the club slowly began to return to normal after all the excitement. Malcolm sat behind his desk and blocked out everyone else talking and being utterly confused.

"Malcolm!" Vanity called as she walked up beside his desk, drawing his attention away from what he was thinking. "Did Boss tell you what the plan was?"

"The only thing that Boss told me was that this detective dude that works for him is supposed to call me, and I'm supposed to call our father to tell him he needs help!" Malcolm said with a chuckle.

"So what are you going to do?" Vanity asked him.

"What do you mean, what am I going to do?" Malcolm shot back, staring at Vanity like she was crazy. "I'm not Boss, Vanity! I don't think like Boss, and I don't move like him either. So what exactly do you expect me to be?"

"I expect you to be the Malcolm Warren Jr. you were before Boss ever showed up!" Vanity told him in a tone that not only got his attention but also quieted everyone else. "You asked me what I expect you to do. You're not Boss. Yeah, that may be true. But last I checked, the same blood that flows through his veins flows through yours, and you've been around and dealt with Boss long enough to know what Boss expects from his brother, not me! My only question is, what are you going to do?"

Malcolm stared into Vanity's eyes a moment, only to slowly smile and then give a light laugh. He first called to Trigger and then to Moses and Savage, getting the attention of all three men.

"I hope you three are ready to put in work, because until my brother is out, we about to bleed the streets!"

"That's what the fuck I'm talking about!" Trigger stated, rubbing his hands together with his devilish smile on his face.

Vanity slowly smiled as she stood staring down at Malcolm Jr. She then met his eyes when he looked back up at her, showing a smirk on his lips that reminded her of Boss.

16

Boss sat through five hours of questioning and bullshit from the FBI, only to deal with the ATF immediately afterward. He sat through it all calmly and quietly, giving both agencies the same response—not a muthafucking thing, which infuriated the agents. In return, he received threat after threat from life in prison to the death sentence. But Boss just sat and smirked at both lead agents.

After he was finished with the questioning and threats, Boss was finally processed and fingerprinted. He was then given an orange jumpsuit with Miami DC Jail written across the back, along with a pair of blue step-in shoes. He was then transferred up to the fourth floor, which was supposed to be a high-security area. He followed the correctional guard into the dormitory-like jail unit.

"Stay here, Holmes!"

Boss looked at the male guard for a brief moment as he entered the booth where the officer sat inside. He looked back out over the floor and saw different inmates, some of whom were staring back at him as they all moved around the day room either watching television or playing a table game.

Boss walked further into the unit and looked around some more. He peeped the phone area, just as one inmate was hanging up one of the six phones.

He headed over to an open phone. Boss was just about to pick it up, when his name was yelled out, which drew his attention to his left side, where he saw the guard he had arrived with along with another tall, stocky guard with a clean-shaven head walking his way.

"Boy! Is you hard of fucking hearing or something?" the guard asked, stopping right up in his face. "I'm sure my officer told your ass to stay by the door!"

Boss made a show of looking around as if he was trying to see who the guard was talking to. He then looked back at him and stared him in the eyes.

"You talking to me, playboy?"

"You think you're funny, huh?" the guard asked with a small sneaky smile. "I think I'ma like you being here, boy! Hang up the damn phone and come with me!"

"Let me get that, nigga!" an inmate said, snatching the phone out of Boss's hand and giving him a look. "What, you got a problem?"

"I'll holla at you later!" Boss answered with a light laugh.

~ ~ ~

Boss waited while listening to the bullshit that a stocky guard named Sergeant Moon was telling him. The sergeant also threw in some indirect threats at Boss as to what could happen to him. Boss just sat quietly, already deciding he would have to get rid of the sergeant, seeing the problem only getting worse the longer he had to be inside the jail. He received what was supposed to be a bedroll and was given his room assignment. Boss then was allowed to leave the officer station, so he headed straight to the phone area, where two phones were open. He walked over to the one in the corner next to the plexi-glass window that overlooked the outdoor recreation yard.

"Naw, my nigga!" an inmate said, snatching up the phone before Boss could pick up the headset.

Boss shifted his eyes to the face of the inmate that grabbed the phone, and he instantly recognized him from earlier. Boss gave him a small smile.

"You find something—!"

Boss never gave the inmate a chance to finish what he

was saying. He hit him in the throat before homeboy realized it, and while the inmate was choking, Boss smashed the inmate's face into the plexi-glass window. While he was falling face-first to the ground, Boss picked up the hanging headphone to make his call. He ignored the way the other inmates around him were now staring at him.

"Boss?"

"Yeah, ma! I'm here. You good?"

"What do you think, Boss? Are you with me right now?"

Boss didn't bother answering her.

"You still at the club or penthouse?"

"Home, Boss!" Vanity told him, sounding a little aggravated. "I've spoken with your father and your lawyer. We tried to bond you out, but you have a federal hold on you."

"I already knew that was going to happen. Do me a favor though, ma. Call my brother on a three-way."

"Hold on!"

Boss looked down on the floor at the inmate who was beginning to wake up. He shook his head but focused back on his call when he heard the third line ringing.

"Babe, you there?"

"Yeah, Vanity!" Boss replied.

"What's up, Vanity?" Malcolm answered his phone.

"Malcolm, Boss is on the phone!" Vanity told him.

"Baby Brother!"

"Yeah!" Boss replied. "You heard from that person I told you about yet?"

"Yeah! He says he's still looking into that, but when everything is everything, you already know what's what, baby Brother! I called Dad, and he's on his way down here too!"

"That's what up!" Boss said before he switched to speaking in code, telling Malcolm a few things he needed his brother to know.

"I got that, baby Brother! Don't worry about what's out here!" Malcolm told his brother. "You good in there?"

"Yeah. Oh wait!" Boss said, remembering his little problem.

He spoke in code and told Malcolm what he wanted done to Sergeant Moon.

Once the call had ended, Boss hung up the headset and left the phone area. He headed toward the stairs, when he spotted the homeboy he had put to sleep. He then saw

Sergeant Moon walk out of the officers' station. Boss began to walk up the stairs, when he heard the sergeant yell his name. Boss stopped and turned back around to face the sergeant.

"Do you always yell, or is it that you get off at yelling at a grown-ass man?" Boss asked the sergeant before he could say shit.

"You really are going to learn about that slick-ass mouth of yours!" Sergeant Moon told Boss.

The sergeant began to say more, only for Boss to beat him to it.

"You'll learn who it is you're dealing with!"

Sergeant Moon watched the inmate walk up the stairs. He smiled since he already had some big plans for inmate ReSean Holmes.

17

After Boss's arrest and finding out that the government was charging him with everything from trafficking to kingpin shit, both Malcolm Sr. and Malcolm Jr. used every connect they had. They tried to find answers that could help them get Boss out of jail and keep him from going to prison.

By the fourth week of Boss's incarceration, and after appearing before a judge for the fifth time, Malcolm Jr. finally got some good news. He heard from Detective Aaron Wright, who told him that they needed to meet.

"Where and when?" Malcolm asked the hired detective.

He then sat back a few moments and listened as the detective gave him directions to the meeting location and time they were to meet.

As soon as he hung up with the detective, Malcolm called Moses as he was snatching up his keys and burner from his office desktop.

"What's up, Malcolm?" Moses asked, walking into his office.

"We leaving!" Malcolm told his friend and bodyguard as

he was walking out of the office door.

He explained to Moses about the meeting as the two of them walked downstairs in his mini-mansion.

Malcolm reached his front door and stepped outside just in time to see the Maybach and two Mercedes trucks pull up in front of his house. Malcolm knew instantly that it was his father. He simply walked over to the Maybach and climbed into the back of the car while Moses got in front next to Ike, his father's best friend and bodyguard.

"What the hell are you doing, boy?" Malcolm Jr. heard his father say. "We about to meet up with Boss's detective connect. We may now have the answer we've been waiting for to all this bullshit with Boss being locked up."

~ ~ ~

Malcolm Jr. pulled up in front of a store that he recognized as the M&M Store. Once the Maybach parked and he got out, not bothering to wait for Moses to open the car door, he looked up and saw a man approaching.

"You look just like my main man!" the man told Malcolm Jr. as he walked up on him.

"Who the fuck is you?" Moses asked while standing right beside Malcolm.

"Name's Berry!" the guy replied to Moses and Malcolm. "I work for Boss."

"What's your position with my son?" Malcolm Sr. spoke up as he and Ike walked around the back end of the Maybach and stared at the man.

"Well, I'll be damned!" Berry said, smiling as he stared at the two familiar faces. "If it ain't the O.G. Malcolm Warren himself! You say Boss is your son, huh?"

"Who are you?" Malcolm Jr. spoke up.

"As I said before, I work for Boss, and my loyalty is only to Boss. Because he was the one that gave ol' Berry a chance; and whatever ol' Berry has to do for Boss, ol' Berry will do. So with that said, you all have a meeting with another one of Boss's people that works for him! Follow me!"

Malcolm Jr. looked at his father with a confused look, but he soon followed before anyone else knew it. He followed him from the parking lot and into the store, where he saw Berry nod to the guy behind the counter before disappearing behind it himself. Malcolm Jr. then looked back to see his father, Ike, and Moses all following him.

"Right here!" Berry said, stopping in front of a closed door down a long hallway.

He opened the door, and then motioned for the others to step inside.

Malcolm Jr. went to step inside first; however, Moses grabbed his arm and walked in before him. Malcolm Jr. then followed his bodyguard into the room where he saw a brown-skinned man sitting at a fold-out table with what looked like a black folder in front of him.

"Well, look who's decided to show up to the party!" Detective Wright said, smiling at the infamous Malcolm Warren Sr. "Malcolm Warren himself!"

"You Detective Aaron Wright?" Malcolm Jr. asked him.

"I am!" he replied. "I have what we need to free Boss. But it's going to take some work getting to this witness, because he's being protected by the FBI as we speak!"

"Let's see what you got, Detective!" Malcolm Sr. spoke up as he stepped forward.

Detective Wright pushed the folder across the desk, only for Malcolm Jr. to pick it up first.

He opened the folder and first saw a photo on top. Malcolm Jr. stared at the picture before hearing his father speak up.

"This is the guy that's the witness for the Feds. His name

is Tim Wilson!"

"This is the person that—!"

"Shot me!" Malcolm Jr. finished the detective's sentence for him, recognizing the guy in the photo. "This is the muthafucka that tried to kill me!"

"What?" both Malcolm Sr. and Moses said.

Malcolm Jr. nodded his head.

"Yeah! This is the punk muthafucka! I recognize the tattoo on this fuckin' nigga's neck!" he explained.

~ ~ ~

Vanity was looking over some paperwork from her club when the phone rang on top of the coffee table to her right. She picked it up and answered.

"Hello!"

She smiled when she heard it was a collect call from Boss. She pressed the number 5 and accepted the call.

"Hey, you!"

"What's up, ma? You good?"

"I miss you, but I'm just looking over a few papers from the club. How are you doing in there?"

"I'm doing!" Boss admitted to her. "Do me a favor though, ma. Call my brother for me real quick."

"Hold on a sec, babe!" Vanity told Boss as she clicked over to another line and called Malcolm Jr.

Once the line began ringing, Vanity connected both lines.

"Boss, you there, babe?"

"Yeah, I'm here, ma!"

"Yeah!" Malcolm Jr. answered the phone. "Who the fuck is this?"

"Hey, big Brother! What's up with you?"

"Boss?"

"Yeah! What's going on with you, playboy?"

"Yo! Hold on!" Malcolm Jr. told his brother.

"I wonder what's wrong with him?" Vanity asked Boss.

"I'm about to find out in a minute!" Boss said, just as another voice came over the phone. "Boss, you there?"

"Yeah, Pops. What's up?"

"Son, listen! We're going to take care of this problem tonight! Nothing else needs to be said after this. Are we understood?"

"Perfectly, Pops!"

After hearing the line hang up, Vanity spoke up and called to Boss.

"Yeah, ma!" Boss answered. "You at home you say, right?"

"Yes, Boss! Why?"

"I want you to stay inside until you hear from me, okay?"

"Boss, what's going on?"

"If I know my father at least a little bit now, I think I'm about to come home. But I need you to be where I can reach you and know you're safe."

"All right, babe!"

Vanity continued her conversation with Boss until their time ended and the phone hung up. She sat back for a few moments thinking, when her phone rang again.

"Hello!"

"Vanity, it's Steffaine."

"Hey, Steffaine, girl. What's up?"

"You speak to Boss lately?"

"Actually, I just hung up with him. Why, what's wrong?"

"I just got a call from Malcolm!"

"Let me guess!" Vanity interrupted her. "Malcolm told you to stay inside the house, didn't he?"

"Vanity, what's going on?"

"Girl, knowing Boss and Malcolm, there's about to be

something going down, and I'm sure it has to do with getting Boss out of jail!"

~ ~ ~

Malcolm Jr. got Trigger, Savage, Princess, and Black Widow together as Moses explained to them what was going on. The four members of Boss's crew were not surprised at the plan and were ready to do whatever was necessary to get their leader out of jail.

Malcolm Jr. had the location where the FBI was hiding Tim Wilson. He sat in the passenger seat of the Yukon truck, along with the other five members of the crew packed inside. They were completely quiet as Moses drove out of Miami Dade County and headed to Fort Lauderdale.

Once they arrived in Fort Lauderdale, Malcolm Jr. pulled out his phone and made a quick call.

"Agent Miller!"

"We're ten minutes away!" Malcolm said into the phone.

"Yes sir! There are two assigned agents with me, sir, and we also have backup in a dark blue Malibu, sir. When should we expect you. Ten minutes, you say?"

"Leave the back door open!" Malcolm told the agent that was being paid a lot of money to help them get to Tim

Wilson.

Princess and Black Widow walked back up the street twelve minutes later after quietly dealing with the two FBI agents that were parked two houses away from the same house where Tim Wilson was being kept inside. Both agents had been killed in the backup Malibu. Malcolm then heard the back doors of the Yukon open, and felt the shifting of the truck as Savage and Trigger got out and disappeared around the back of the safe house.

Malcolm's eyes locked up on the twin sisters as the two of them walked up the walkway and headed toward the front door. He watched as one of the sisters knocked on the front door and waited until it was opened. A white male agent stood at the doorway and smiled as the two women flirted with him.

"Here we go!" Moses announced, seeing the agent at the front door spin around to look behind him.

Malcolm Jr. watched the swiftness that both Princess and Black Widow showed as they pulled out their burners with silencers attached. There was not a sound when the back of the agent's head was blown off, with blood flying everywhere. Malcolm sat waiting for a few minutes until finally Princess and Black Widow exited the safe house followed a short time later by Trigger and then Savage, who was carrying a body across his shoulders.

Once the four of them were back inside the Yukon with the supposed witness on the floor, Malcolm Jr. nodded to Moses and then called over to Trigger.

"What's up, Malcolm?" Trigger answered as he glanced down at the knocked out Tim Wilson.

"The agent. What happened?" Malcolm asked, looking back at Trigger.

"It went as planned!" Trigger replied. "We took the snitch, killed everyone but the agent, and only hit him two times. One shot to the chest, since he was wearing a vest, and one shot in the upper side shoulder area. We left him lying across the sofa."

Malcolm Jr. nodded his head in approval. He then pulled out his phone and made another phone call.

"Is it finished?" Malcolm Sr. asked, after answering the phone call.

"Everything's finished. We're on our way to the ware-house now!"

"I'll meet you all there," Malcolm Sr. told his son before

he hung up.

~ ~ ~

Malcolm Sr. made another call after hanging up with his oldest son. He stood out on the terrace of his penthouse and listened to the line ring.

"Attorney Summers!"

"Faith, it's Malcolm."

"Hello, Mr. Warren. What can I do for you?"

"I apologize for calling at this hour, but I have a few questions for you concerning my son, ReSean."

"Okay, Mr. Warren. I'm listening."

"Exactly how much does the government have on my son?"

"Truthfully, Mr. Warren, the case against ReSean is only strengthened by this witness the FBI has, because everything else is too weak to hold against your son. There was never any proof to point anything at ReSean. So, again, the only thing that's strong enough to convict him is this witness!"

"So without this witness, how long can they hold these charges against my son?"

"With no witness, Mr. Warren, this case will end up being dismissed within days!"

"That's what I wanted to know!" Malcolm Sr. stated, smiling after hearing what his son's attorney had to tell him.

18

Boss was escorted through the jail after a three-hour wait once his charges were dropped and his case dismissed for lack of evidence. Even though it wasn't mentioned while court was still in session, it was worldwide news that the government's star witness was suspected to have died. Boss ignored all the stares he was receiving from inmates as well as police officers and jail guards. He walked out of the front door of the Miami-Dade County Jail to the flashes of cameras and a huge crowd of reporters with cameras all yelling out questions.

He quickly noticed the most gorgeous face among the crowd as men dressed in all black quickly made a pathway through the mass of people. Boss recognized a few of the faces when he glanced around, but he was mainly focused on only two people who stood in front of the Rolls-Royce Wraith that was parked in front of the courthouse, in the middle of the street. He walked down the steps with a big smile on his face and straight up to Vanity, who stood smiling back at him.

"What's up, ma?" Boss questioned, once he stopped in front of Vanity and smiled down at her.

"You!" she replied as she threw her arms up around her man's neck and leaned in to kiss his lips.

Boss broke the kiss after a few minutes as they smiled into each other's eyes. He finally released his hold on Vanity and then looked over at his brother and met his eyes.

"What's up, big Brother? I see you came through for me!"

"Why wouldn't I? We brothers!" Malcolm told Boss as the two of them embraced in a tight brotherly bond.

"I've got a special gift for you, baby Brother!" Malcolm whispered into Boss's ear before they ended their hug.

Boss gave Malcolm a look before he turned and followed Vanity into the back of the Rolls-Royce. Malcolm then shut the door behind the two of them as he walked back to his Mercedes S-Class where Moses was waiting.

"So, how does it feel?" Vanity asked as she wrapped her arm around Boss, lying into his side with her head against his chest.

"I missed you, so that should answer your question, ma!" Boss told her, causing Vanity to lift her head up and smile at him before kissing him on the lips.

"You do know Malcolm is planning something, right?" Vanity told Boss.

She then picked up her Louis Vuitton bag, dug inside, and pulled out an already rolled phat blunt. She handed it over to Boss along with his personal gold lighter that she had bought for him.

"Good looking out, ma!" Boss said, smiling at the sight of the blunt. "Malcolm did tell me he had something for me. You know what he's talking about?"

"Nope!" Vanity answered. "I think it has something to do with your father, since I saw him and Malcolm Jr. talking before we left to come and get you."

"We'll see once we get there, I guess!" Boss replied, and then called up front to Trigger and Princess. "What's good, family?"

"What up, big Bruh?"

"Hey, pretty boy!"

Trigger and Princess smiled back at Boss. They were both happy to see him back where he belonged.

~ ~ ~

Boss recognized the warehouse and saw the rest of his

team all crowded out in front. He waited until the Rolls-Royce was parked and his door was opened before he climbed out to the sound of cheering and yelling as his team welcomed him home.

He waited until Vanity climbed out behind him. He took her hand, and then the two of them walked into the crowd of his people, who had helped build up his business and fight for him to get to where they all were now. He allowed his team to show their love until he stopped face-to-face with his father, who had his boy, Ike, standing right next to him with a huge smile on his face.

"What's up, Pops?" Boss said as he smiled and held his father's eyes.

"Welcome home, Son!" Malcolm Sr. said to him, slowly smiling as he embraced his youngest son in a fatherly hug. "We've got something for you!"

"So I've been told!" Boss replied after his father released him.

He took Vanity's hand back into his and then followed behind his father and brother as the two of them led the way over to the warehouse entrance, where two of Malcolm Jr.'s men opened the doors.

"Come over here, Boss!" Malcolm Sr. told his son as he and his oldest son stood in front of the man that was tied to a chair in the center of the warehouse with a hood covering his head.

"Who's this?" Boss asked as he walked up to stand at his father's right side.

"This is the muthafucka that was working with the Feds!" Malcolm Jr. informed his brother, standing to the left of his father. "He's also the punk muthafucka that tried to body my ass, Boss!"

Boss said nothing else. He simply walked over to the guy and pulled off the hood. But he paused a moment a little surprised after recognizing the man in front of him.

"Yo, Eazy! Come here for a second, fam!"

"What's up, fam?" Eazy said as he walked up beside Boss and stared down at the guy in front of him.

"You know who this is, right?" Boss asked, looking over at Eazy.

"Yeah!" Eazy answered with a small smile. "This is that nigga Tim from the shop that Erica worked at. He's Brandi's cousin."

"I thought so!" Boss stated as he pulled the gag from

Tim's mouth, only for the boy to spit at him.

"Trigger!" Boss called out, just as his boy instantly appeared at Boss's side with his burner gripped inside his hand. "It's cool, baby Bruh!"

After Trigger fell back only a step, Boss turned his attention back to Tim.

"I'm not going to ask you why, because I'm sure it's because you let your evil-ass cousin fill your head up with her bullshit. But I'll tell you what! I'm not going to kill you!" Boss calmly said.

Boss heard the protests from his team who were all standing around him. They were all watching and certainly expected to see Boss murder Tim. Instead, Boss held up his hand to quiet everyone. He then looked at Malcolm Jr. and whispered something to his brother that got Malcolm to slowly begin to smile.

Boss turned away from Tim and then walked back over to his father.

Boom! Boom! Boom! Boom!

Boss didn't bother turning around to see what had happened behind him, since he already knew after just giving his brother permission to get a little payback for what Tim had done to him.

"How about we all get out of here now and get something to eat? I'm hungry as hell, Pops!" Boss said as he met his father's smiling eyes.

19

Three days after his father had left to fly back to Chicago to get back to business, Boss got back to his own business as well. He and Malcolm Jr. first sat down together to discuss combining their organizations to make one larger group. The two easily and quickly agreed, and then they decided they would get both parties together to have a sit-down and discuss the new decision that was made.

The next morning, Boss called Detective Wright and set up a meeting for noon at the club. He then stopped by Collins Smokehouse to speak with Evelyn and Mr. Collins about meeting with the detective and getting permission from them. However before he could leave, Mrs. Collins forced him and Trigger to stay and have some lunch.

When Detective Wright showed up at the club, Trigger escorted him to the back office where Boss was on the phone with Vanity. Boss hung up after noticing the detective and stood up to shake his hand.

"Glad to see you're back home!" Detective Wright told Boss as the two of them sat down across from each other.

"It's good to be home!" Boss replied, just as Trigger appeared in the doorway with a Louis Vuitton duffel bag.

Boss then nodded his thanks to Trigger, took the bag from him, and tossed it over to the detective.

"Two million dollars as I promised!"

"Wow!" Detective Wright cried in shock, smiling as he stared down at the bag. "I've never seen this type of cash before!"

"Now I need you to do one more thing, Cop!"

"I'm listening."

"Now that you're a millionaire, I don't need you just quitting the force!" Boss told him. "You can make a lot more money staying with the police force and sticking with me."

"I'll be truthfully honest with you, Boss," the detective began. "It's becoming harder to move around with this new sergeant on my back."

Boss pulled out his phone and made a call.

"Yeah, Boss!" Malcolm Sr. answered.

"Pops, I need a favor."

"What's up?"

"Hold on!" Boss told his father as he looked back at the detective. "What's the sergeant's name?"

"Howard Butler," Detective Wright told Boss in disbelief.

"Pops!"

"Yeah, son? What's up?"

"I need you to pull some strings with your mayor friend, and I need you to get a Sergeant Howard Butler transferred or whatever. But see if you can get a promotion to sergeant for my detective friend."

"What's the detective's name?"

"Aaron Wright?"

"I'll see what I can do!"

After hanging up with his father, Boss looked back at the detective.

"Are there any more problems?"

"We're all clear!" Detective Wright told Boss.

The detective could only smile as he shook his head in complete disbelief at the young man sitting in front of him.

~ ~ ~

"I'm coming!" Steffaine yelled as she was coming down the stairs after hearing the doorbell ring.

She made it to the front door just as whoever was on the other side rang the bell over and over. Steffaine looked out the peephole and saw that it was Malcolm Jr.

"Boy, what's wrong with your ass?" Steffaine asked after quickly snatching open the front door.

"I'm tired of you ignoring me!" Malcolm Jr. answered her as he walked past her into the penthouse.

"Excuse you!" Steffaine said, following Malcolm with her eyes. "I don't remember inviting you in, Malcolm!"

Steffaine sucked her teeth when she was ignored, but she closed and then locked the front door behind her. She then followed Malcolm into the den, where he was already seated on her sofa with the TV remote in his hand and his feet thrown up onto her coffee table. She walked over and pushed his feet down.

"What are you doing here, Malcolm? What do you want?" she asked with a lot of attitude.

"You!" Malcolm boldly told her as he sat looking up at her. "It's been months, and you still refuse to answer my question."

"What question?"

"About us, woman! Quit playing with me, Steffaine!"

"Have you ever stopped to consider that maybe I'm not interested in you or a relationship with anybody?" Steffaine asked, staring down at Malcolm with her hands on her hips.

Malcolm slowly smiled up at her before he stood to his feet, and then looked down into her eyes.

"So you're not interested in me or a relationship with me, Steffaine?"

"Mal—!"

Steffaine was unable to finish what she was saying as Malcolm bent down and kissed her on the lips. She felt herself quickly getting caught up in the passionate and sex-hungered kiss. She then felt Malcolm pick her up as she wrapped her legs around his waist and her arms around his neck to deepen the kiss.

~ ~ ~

"Oh God! Yessss, Malcolm!" Steffaine screamed out in passion.

She straddled him and rode the hell out of him, feeling him deep inside of her. She rode him faster and faster, slamming down onto his manhood as she easily hit her spot, feeling herself close to exploding.

Malcolm allowed Steffaine to get hers first, since he had plans for her once she got what she thought was her only orgasm. He felt the walls of her pussy tighten around his dick, and he listened as she grew louder with her cries until she screamed his name and finally began to cum. He caught her before she fell over while still cumming. Malcolm then flipped her over onto her back without slipping out of her.

He immediately got to work and focused on getting Steffaine to orgasm again. Malcolm then sexed her in different positions while listening to her scream his name and beg him to cum, only to cry out that she was cumming again herself. He smiled through it all.

"Who's it belong to, Steffaine?" he demanded from her as he lay chest to back on top of her as he slowly ground into her from the back while whispering into her ear. "Is this my pussy or what?"

"Is that all you want?" Steffaine got out between moans while gripping the pillow under her head.

"You know I want you!" Malcolm told her as he continued slowly grinding into her, pushing deeper and getting her to scream out his name. "I'm trying to make you mine, Steffaine. Are you going to give me what I want?"

"Malcolm!" Steffaine cried. "I swear, if you play or hurt me! Oh God, yes! I'm going to kill you if you hurt me, Malcolm!"

"That's not my plan, baby!" Malcolm told her as he kissed the side of her head, just as she cried that she was about to cum again but begging him to cum with her.

"Will you give me what I want?" he asked as he ground a little faster and pushed deeper inside her.

"Yes! Yes, Malcolm! I'll be your woman, baby! Just please cum for me!" she begged.

"Gladly!" Malcolm replied with a smile.

~ ~ ~

After showering together after their love-making and lying together in her bed, Malcolm lay listening to Steffaine admit to him about the last guy she was seeing and how he wasn't the man she thought he was supposed to be. No one knew it, but he beat her. Malcolm just listened to her, when his phone began to ring. He was going to ignore it, but Steffaine told him to answer it.

"What's up, baby Brother?" Malcolm said, after seeing that Boss was calling.

"Malcolm, we got a problem, big Brother! Where you at?"

"I'm at Steffaine's spot! What's up, though?"

"Not over the phone! Meet me at the penthouse and bring

Steffaine with you. Vanity wants to holla at her anyway."

After hanging up with Boss, Malcolm looked over at Steffaine.

"Baby, what's wrong? What's Boss talking about now?"

"I'm not sure yet, but we need to drive over to the penthouse," he told her. "Vanity wants to talk to you about something."

~ ~ ~

Boss waited for about twenty minutes after hanging up with his brother, when he finally heard their voices inside the penthouse from behind him. He stood out on the roof terrace smoking a blunt and drinking. Boss looked back over his shoulder to see Malcolm Jr. walk out onto the roof.

"What's up, baby Brother?" Malcolm said as he and Boss embraced each other. "What's this new problem already?"

"You remember Steven Wallace?" Boss asked as he passed the blunt over to Malcolm.

"Let me guess!" Malcolm said before taking a pull from the blunt and blowing out a cloud of thick weed smoke. "Big brother, Daniels Wallace finally showed up?"

Boss nodded his head yes and then took a sip of his rum

and Coke.

"Homeboy left us a message at the club!"

"What's the message?"

"Surrender or start to prepare for a war!"

Malcolm laughed lightly as he shook his head after listening to what his little brother had just told him.

"So let me guess, baby Brother. You ready to go to war with this dude, ain't you?" Malcolm stated.

"Truthfully, big Brother!" Boss began as he took the blunt back from Malcolm. "I can't see us making no money with all this war we keep getting into."

"Well then, make sure this is the last one and muthafuckas know that this shit isn't a game to be played with or tested!" Malcolm said to his brother.

Malcolm watched as Boss nodded his head, and then he saw the familiar look appear on his younger's brother's face.

20

Boss and Malcolm did not respond to the message left by Daniels Wallace, which was a clear and loud enough response to the guy to let him know that if war was what he wanted, then he could bring it. Both Boss and Malcolm were smart enough to tighten up security more than it already had been, and they placed more guards around Vanity, Steffaine, and Gigi. They even accepted help from Rachell, who had heard about Boss's problem, so she sent her men to assist him as well.

Boss also got with the connect Vanity had introduced to him who supplied them with whatever types of weapons they needed. The guy also just happened to be Vanity's stepbrother, who she had never told him about until recently. Boss and Malcolm also made sure each man on the team had firepower and backup. Even Vanity, Steffaine, and Gigi had bangers just in case.

Two weeks after the initial warning, Daniels Wallace and his men made their first attack, catching Eazy and Butter in the middle of a pickup and drop-off. Malcolm had heard about the shoot-out first, and with a team of fifteen, he was able to back up his boys. Unknown by Daniels, his location had been revealed to Boss by Sergeant Wright, who had a few men on the lookout for him.

Boss then responded in the middle of the night right after the attempt on Eazy and Butter. He sent a hit team out to the Hollywood Oaks rental house that he was told was being rented by Wallace. Boss and his men left the house shot up with four dead inside, but Daniels was nowhere inside the house.

After hearing about the wasted attempt, Boss contacted Sergeant Wright.

"Cop, what the hell was this information you gave me?" Boss barked as soon as Sergeant Wright was on the phone.

"I've already heard about what happened, Boss," Wright told him. "Relax! I'm already on it, and so far, it's looking like this guy Wallace is connected."

"You mean he's got somebody inside the department too?"

"I'm guessing!"

"You guessing?" Boss yelled. "I'm not paying you all this money to guess, Cop. Find this muthafucka!"

~ ~ ~

Daniels Wallace picked up his ringing phone as he sat in

front of the television watching the news in another house he had rented. He looked from the television screen to the cell phone and recognized the name and number.

"What up, Butler?" Daniels answered.

"How are you?"

"Thanks to your warning, I'm still alive!"

"I told you this kid wasn't your normal kid, Daniels. We have to be really careful with this move against him."

"What about his brother, Malcolm Warren Jr.?" Daniels asked. "How much trouble is he going to be?"

"That one is the weaker of the two!" Butler told Daniels. "If we get this Boss kid out of the picture, then everyone and everything else will fall. Boss is our main focus and should be our first target!"

Daniels agreed with Butler's idea on dealing directly with Boss. The two spoke for a few more minutes before Daniels hung up and made another phone call.

"Yeah!"

"Kobe, I may need you after all out here in Miami! This boy, Boss as he's called, has proven to be a little more than I expected. Also, bring more men with you, because these boys play hard out here, cousin!"

"I'm on my way!"

~ ~ ~

Malcolm heard the knock at the front door as he and Steffaine were eating in the den. He motioned for her to continue to eat as he stood up and headed for the front door. Malcolm saw Boss and the crew through the peephole, so he unlocked the door and opened it.

"What's up, baby Brother?" Malcolm asked as he stepped back and allowed Boss, Trigger, Eazy, and the rest of the crew into the penthouse.

"Why you not answering your phone?" Boss asked as he stepped into the den and saw Steffaine looking over at him.

"We gotta talk!"

"I've got some work to finish up!" Steffaine informed them as she walked up beside Malcolm.

She went up onto her toes and kissed him on the lips. She then winked at Boss before she turned and headed upstairs.

Malcolm watched Steffaine a few moments as she headed up the stairs. He then looked back at Boss.

"I see you two finally decided to stop with the bullshit!" Boss said.

Malcolm smirked at Boss and then nodded for the others to come into the den.

Once everyone was seated and Black Widow was picking up the fried chicken wing from Malcolm's plate,

Malcolm began to speak directly to Boss.

"So, what's the problem, baby brother?"

"Have you been watching the news?" Boss asked his brother. "We got a problem, because this dude, Daniels Wallace, is a little smarter than we guess him to be. Cop says he thinks this guy has some connects inside the department, because his ass got missing before we hit this rental house where he was supposed to be laid up in at three o'clock in the morning!"

"So basically you saying we missed this clown?" Malcolm asked, seeing Boss nod his head. "You got cop checking to see who this connect is?"

Boss nodded his head again.

"But there's one thing this clown Daniels slipped up on!"

"What's that?" Malcolm inquired as he looked over at Trigger.

"He left muthafuckas behind who are willing to talk once they see Savage walk into the warehouse."

Malcolm looked over at Savage and saw the big, dreadlocked man and the expression on his face as he sat staring straight back at him. Malcolm then looked at Boss and saw Princess whisper something to him.

"So, what is it we got, Boss?"

Boss shifted his eyes back to his brother as Princess

finished saying something to him.

"From what we were able to get out of this guy who worked for Daniels, our friend not only has a wife and son back in Orlando, but he also has a mother and father in Orlando who he left behind to come out here to die for nothing!"

"So, what's up? When we leaving?" Malcolm asked with a smile.

"We not!" Boss told his brother, watching the smile slowly fade from his lips. "You're leaving for Orlando—tonight!"

To be continued . . .

Text Good2Go at 31996 to receive new release
updates via text message.

To order books, please fill out the order form below:
To order films please go to www.good2gofilms.com

Name:_____

Address:_____

City: _____ State: _____ Zip Code: _____

Phone:_____

Email:_____

Method of Payment: Check   VISA   MASTERCARD

Credit Card#:_____

Name as it appears on card: _____

Signature: _____

Item Name	Price	Qty	Amount
48 Hours to Die – Silk White	$14.99		
A Hustler's Dream - Ernest Morris	$14.99		
A Hustler's Dream 2 - Ernest Morris	$14.99		
A Thug's Devotion – J.L.Rose & J.M.McMillon	$14.99		
Black Reign – Ernest Morris	$14.99		
Bloody Mayhem Down South	$14.99		
Business Is Business – Silk White	$14.99		
Business Is Business 2 – Silk White	$14.99		
Business Is Business 3 – Silk White	$14.99		
Childhood Sweethearts – Jacob Spears	$14.99		
Childhood Sweethearts 2 – Jacob Spears	$14.99		
Childhood Sweethearts 3 - Jacob Spears	$14.99		
Childhood Sweethearts 4 - Jacob Spears	$14.99		
Connected To The Plug – Dwan Marquis Williams	$14.99		
Connected To The Plug 2 – Dwan Marquis Williams	$14.99		
Connected To The Plug 3 – Dwan Williams	$14.99		
Deadly Reunion – Ernest Morris	$14.99		
Flipping Numbers – Ernest Morris	$14.99		
Flipping Numbers 2 – Ernest Morris	$14.99		
He Loves Me, He Loves You Not - Mychea	$14.99		
He Loves Me, He Loves You Not 2 - Mychea	$14.99		
He Loves Me, He Loves You Not 3 - Mychea	$14.99		
He Loves Me, He Loves You Not 4 – Mychea	$14.99		

He Loves Me, He Loves You Not 5 – Mychea	$14.99		
Lord of My Land – Jay Morrison	$14.99		
Lost and Turned Out – Ernest Morris	$14.99		
Married To Da Streets – Silk White	$14.99		
M.E.R.C. - Make Every Rep Count Health and Fitness	$14.99		
Money Make Me Cum – Ernest Morris	$14.99		
My Besties – Asia Hill	$14.99		
My Besties 2 – Asia Hill	$14.99		
My Besties 3 – Asia Hill	$14.99		
My Besties 4 – Asia Hill	$14.99		
My Boyfriend's Wife - Mychea	$14.99		
My Boyfriend's Wife 2 – Mychea	$14.99		
My Brothers Envy – J. L. Rose	$14.99		
My Brothers Envy 2 – J. L. Rose	$14.99		
My Brothers Envy 3 – J. L. Rose	$14.99		
Naughty Housewives – Ernest Morris	$14.99		
Naughty Housewives 2 – Ernest Morris	$14.99		
Naughty Housewives 3 – Ernest Morris	$14.99		
Naughty Housewives 4 – Ernest Morris	$14.99		
Never Be The Same – Silk White	$14.99		
Stranded – Silk White	$14.99		
Slumped – Jason Brent	$14.99		
Someone's Gonna Get It – Mychea	$14.99		
Summer's Dirty Little Secret – Ernest Morris	$14.99		
Supreme & Justice – Ernest Morris	$14.99		
Supreme & Justice 2 – Ernest Morris	$14.99		
Supreme & Justice 3 – Ernest Morris	$14.99		
Tears of a Hustler - Silk White	$14.99		
Tears of a Hustler 2 - Silk White	$14.99		
Tears of a Hustler 3 - Silk White	$14.99		
Tears of a Hustler 4- Silk White	$14.99		
Tears of a Hustler 5 – Silk White	$14.99		

Tears of a Hustler 6 – Silk White	$14.99		
The Panty Ripper - Reality Way	$14.99		
The Panty Ripper 3 – Reality Way	$14.99		
The Solution – Jay Morrison	$14.99		
The Teflon Queen – Silk White	$14.99		
The Teflon Queen 2 – Silk White	$14.99		
The Teflon Queen 3 – Silk White	$14.99		
The Teflon Queen 4 – Silk White	$14.99		
The Teflon Queen 5 – Silk White	$14.99		
The Teflon Queen 6 - Silk White	$14.99		
The Vacation – Silk White	$14.99		
Tied To A Boss - J.L. Rose	$14.99		
Tied To A Boss 2 - J.L. Rose	$14.99		
Tied To A Boss 3 - J.L. Rose	$14.99		
Tied To A Boss 4 - J.L. Rose	$14.99		
Tied To A Boss 5 - J.L. Rose	$14.99		
Time Is Money - Silk White	$14.99		
Two Mask One Heart – Jacob Spears and Trayvon Jackson	$14.99		
Two Mask One Heart 2 – Jacob Spears and Trayvon Jackson	$14.99		
Two Mask One Heart 3 – Jacob Spears and Trayvon Jackson	$14.99		
Wrong Place Wrong Time – Silk White	$14.99		
Young Goonz – Reality Way	$14.99		
Subtotal:			
Tax:			
Shipping (Free) U.S. Media Mail:			
Total:			

Make Checks Payable To:
Good2Go Publishing
7311 W Glass Lane
Laveen, AZ 85339

CPSIA information can be obtained
at www.ICGtesting.com
Printed in the USA
LVOW13s1935100118
562549LV00013B/729/P